MW01520273

OTHER WORKS BY BERNARD SLADE

PLAYS

Same Time, Next Year

Tribute

Romantic Comedy

Special Occasions

Fatal Attraction

An Act of the Imagination

Fling!

Return Engagements

You Say Tomatoes

Same Time Another Year

A Very Close Family

I Remember You

Every Time I See You
(musical of Same Time, Next Year)

FILMS

Same Time, Next Year

Tribute

Romantic Comedy

Stand Up and Be Counted

TELEVISION SERIES CREATED

Love on a Rooftop

The Partridge Family

The Flying Nun

Bridget Loves Bernie

Everything Money Can't Buy
(aka Heaven Help Us)

Mr. Deeds Goes to Town

The Bobby Sherman Show

SHARED
LAUGHTER

Shared Laughter

MEMORIES OF

Same Time, Next Year;

The Partridge Family;

Tribute;

The Flying Nun;

Bewitched;

Same Time Another Year;

and other

LAUGHING MATTERS

Bernard Slade

KEY PORTER BOOKS

Canadian Cataloguing in Publication Data

Slade, Bernard, 1930–
    Shared laughter: memories of Same Time, next year; The Partridge family; Tribute;
    The flying nun; Bewitched; Same Time Another Year; and other laughing matters

Includes index.
ISBN 1-55263-308-X

1. Slade, Bernard, 1930– . 2. Dramatists, American – 20th century – Biography. 3. Television comedy writers – United States – Biography. I. Title

PS3569.L2Z476 2000   812'.54   C00-931950-6

THE CANADA COUNCIL | LE CONSEIL DES ARTS
FOR THE ARTS | DU CANADA
SINCE 1957 | DEPUIS 1957

The publisher gratefully acknowledges the support of the Canada Council for the Arts and the Ontario Arts Council for its publishing program.

We acknowledge the financial support of the Government of Canada through the Book Publishing Industry Development Program (BPIDP) for our publishing activities.

Key Porter Books Limited
70 The Esplanade
Toronto, Ontario
Canada M5E 1R2

www.keyporter.com

Electronic formatting: Heidy Lawrance Associates
Design: Peter Maher
All uncredited photographs appear by permission of Bernard Slade

Printed and bound in Canada

00 01 02 03 04   6 5 4 3 2 1

For Jill,
who was there when
all my pages were blank

Contents

Some enchanted evening

It is one o'clock on the morning of March 14, 1975, and a group of about sixteen, consisting of my wife, Jill, our son, Christopher, and friends who have flown in from California and Toronto, are in a room at the Sherry Netherland Hotel waiting for the *New York Times* review of my play *Same Time, Next Year.*

I have been staying at the luxurious Sherry for the rehearsal period because my business manager, Murray Neidorf, in a Brooklyn accent undiminished by thirty years in California, had said, "There will be enough pain. Better you should be comfortable." Another friend had endorsed the decision by pointing out that there was a good bar downstairs and another right across the street at the Plaza. I said, "I don't drink." He said, "You will." I did.

The entire group had attended the opening night performance and the party afterwards at the Picadilly Hotel on Forty-Fifth Street. This noisy, frenetic mass of people had included such notables as Barbara Walters, Art Carney, Marlo Thomas, Lee Strassberg, Sammy Cahn, Leonard Bernstein, and Adolph Green, but the attention of the paparazzi was directed almost solely at the then wife of Gene Saks, Bea Arthur, who was at the peak of her career as the title character in *Maude* and who proceeded to get quite smashed and make grotesque faces at the photographers, who, of course, would splash these images across the front pages of the tabloids the next day.

At one point, seated next to me, she leaned over to talk and made a gesture with her hand, which, in a careless and totally unsexual way, landed squarely on my crotch. My problem was that she left it there. Already bemused by the excitement of the evening, I had no idea what to do about this curious situation. So I did nothing. I mean, what was I to say? "Madame, I'll thank you to remove your hand from my private parts!" No, I simply sat there becoming conscious that my groin was becoming quite warm and moist. Bea seemed quite unaware of the location of her hand, which gave me some pause for thought. In later years our paths would briefly cross professionally, but we were never as physically intimate again.

There were a number of television sets around the room and from time to time, there would be loud applause as the critics broadcast what I gathered were their favorable reviews. I wasn't able to hear these but in the blur of noise and famous faces I do remember seeing our daughter, Laurie, moving back and forth from the public phones, calling a school friend at Sarah Lawrence College who would relay the gist of the notices. I also remember the face of Morton Gottlieb, my producer, floating into a close-up six inches from my nose and yelling, "We've heard the *Times* review is great and it's all about you!" I didn't believe him. I may have been a Broadway neophyte, but I'd been in the business long enough to know not to count your reviews until the ink came off on your hands.

Jill and I escaped the party and, with a couple of friends, drove in Murray's limo up to the Sherry. On the way she told me about the evening's performance, which I hadn't seen, opting to take the coward's way out, stay in the hotel, wash my hair, and play my harmonica, an opening night ritual I've followed ever since. Jill hates first nights too and has said that the epitaph on her tombstone should read: "Died early because she was forced to attend her husband's opening nights." She told me that she had been sitting next to an unidentified critic who, when intermission came, had left his notes on his seat. To avoid the temptation of sneaking a peak she had pushed her way into the crowded lobby to hear Murray saying in a loud voice, to nobody in particular, "Isn't this the best play you've ever seen! Isn't this great! What a wonderful play!" She sidled up to him and said, "Murray, it's a very good play. You don't have to try and *jolly* it into being a hit."

She also gently confided that Charles Grodin, for the first and only time ever, had flubbed one of the funniest and most important lines in the script. This happened because just before the line he got a completely unexpected laugh (probably from an overeager backer), causing him to bury the all-important curtain line. A perfect example of why I protect my heart by not attending opening nights.

Okay, so now we're all gathered at the Sherry, nervously waiting for Clive Barnes's review. Well, Jill and I are nervous … the rest are concentrating on having a good time. Even feeling like an open nerve I can be only mildly annoyed at their behavior as I know it's asking too much for opening night guests to care as deeply about the outcome of my play as I do. My professional life may be hanging in the balance, but they're here to have a party. So everyone is drinking, laughing, joking, and talking about everything but the play, and the noise level is getting dangerously close to attracting complaints from fellow hotel guests when Henry Epstein, the husband of Dasha Epstein, who is one of the principal backers and co-producers of the play, comes through the door. He is holding a newspaper. He says, "Everyone sit down and be quiet!" We arrange ourselves on the bed, the floor, and the chairs and wait.

He reads: "Do not put off till tomorrow what you can do today. Get tickets for *Same Time, Next Year*. It is the funniest comedy about love and adultery to come Broadway's way in years. If that were not enough, it is also touching."

My heart is beating fast, but I also feel oddly disconnected. This isn't about me. This is about Moss Hart.

He reads on to the last paragraph: "What puts the final icing on Mr. Slade's wonderfully confectioned cake is the way in which he contrives to give us a social history of the United States during the past quarter century. His eyes and ear for salient detail are sure, and the period feel is assisted by the evocative use of nostalgic tapes between the scenes. Clever, clever, Mr. Slade. This is an enchanting evening."

Nobody says anything for a long moment. Then the comedy writer Bill Persky breaks the silence: "Look, I don't know if this has anything to do with his review, but I was seated right behind Clive Barnes and just before the curtain went up I turned to my wife and said in a fairly loud voice, 'Isn't it a shame Bern Slade only has six months to live?' I don't know if it helped but ..." He shrugs. The room explodes into laughter.

More champagne is popped and poured. I am hugged a great deal and drink at least a full bottle, which has absolutely no effect upon me. An hour or so later Jill and I go to our bedroom and catch up on the opening night telegrams. As a recent fugitive from television, one of my favorites is from fellow playwright Herb Gardner, which simply says: "No more network story conferences." And then, surprisingly, I fall asleep.

I am awakened by a telephone ringing. It is Morton Gottlieb: "You'd better get down to the theater right away!" I can see through the window that it is snowing. "Why?" I ask. "Because there's a line around the block." Never one to miss a photo opportunity, Morton has a camera record him, dressed in an overcoat, long scarf, and gangster fedora, handing out coffee to the line of waiting ticket buyers. I still have it.

The second phone call is from Richard Avedon, who wants to photograph the cast and me. This is followed by the two phones constantly ringing, with Jill and me running from the bedroom to the living room to field the calls. Again I have the odd feeling that I am in a play about a playwright who has had a smash hit open on Broadway.

Later, Charles, Ellen Burstyn, Gene Saks, and I assemble at Richard Avedon's studio where, all looking tired and winter-white, we pose. The other daily reviews are in and all are enthusiastically positive.

Martin Gottfried, writing in the *Post*, opens with: "It is a pleasure to announce the arrival, last night, of a brand new, bouncing and altogether loveable comedy at the Brooks Atkinson Theater. *Same Time, Next Year* is a very funny romantic play ... genuinely funny and genuinely romantic. It is also honest and true and heartfelt ... a really rewarding entertainment." Despite these accolades the atmosphere is not jubilant but rather subdued. I wish we were all closer so that we could hug one another, pound each other on the back, and yell, "My God, we did it!" but we simply don't have that kind of intimate relationship. Once again, I am struck by the feeling that Chuck and Ellen ... Ellen especially ... have the knack of sucking the joy out of life and turning everything gray.

Outside, on Madison Avenue, I punch Gene on the arm and we grin at one another before I head back to the Sherry, wishing that I liked the actors more.

That night, I drop by the theater to see the Standing Room Only audience. There is the unique buzz of anticipation one only hears in the lobby of a hit show in New York, and I stand there trying to file the sound away in my memory bank. I then watch the performances for a few moments but am now only seeing the flaws and am more conscious of the fact that New Yorkers, by now having been told by the reviews that it's okay to laugh, are doing so from the moment the curtain goes up. I leave, to retreat into the boisterous, comfortable circle of my friends.

People in show business are reputed to be jealous—a favorite story is of two composers who meet at the intermission of a new musical and in answer to the query "What do you think?" the other says, "It's even worse than I'd hoped"—but I do not find that to be true and my friends seem genuinely happy for me. Tonight, at an Italian restaurant, I notice one of them studying me with an odd expression. When I ask him if there's something the matter, he says, "I've just realized … you'll never have to work again!" I take a moment to consider this but then dismiss the idea as fanciful. I'm only forty-four and, no matter how big a hit, this is only one play. But it turns out to be true.

For the next few days I am in a whirl of interviews, including one with a reporter from the *New York Times* who asks what I was doing during the twelve-year gap in my biography in the program. I tell him I was working on shows like *Bewitched,* and creating series like *The Partridge Family* and *The Flying Nun.* When he asks why these weren't mentioned I tell him that I thought the newspapers would pigeonhole me as a California sitcom writer, which would affect the reviews of the play. He says, "That's probably very true."

On March 17, still not down to earth, I look out the window and see the St. Patrick's Day Parade marching up Fifth Avenue. I say to Jill, "Isn't that cute … they're giving me a parade."

"What do you want to do today?" she asks.

I say, "I want to go home."

★ **Timing is all**

My parents were attracted to disasters.

In 1924 they immigrated with my two sisters to Canada and settled nicely in the small town of St. Catharines, Ontario, just in time for the Great Depression. I was born in 1930, and some five years later, as the depression was beginning to wane, they returned to England in time for the onset of World War II. This pattern of ill-timed moves continued throughout the war. The day after war was declared I was evacuated to Brighton to live with a foster family for nine months, but since there was no activity on the "home front" my parents brought me back to London. Three weeks later the Battle of Britain began. My parents, their timing still impeccable, had just rented a house a few blocks from Croydon airport, so we were treated to a worm's-eye view of the aerial dogfights that took place daily in the cloudless late-summer skies. When the daylight raids subsided we moved to the peaceful small town of Caernarvon in North Wales but returned just in time to experience the London blitz. During the lull that followed we relocated to Nottingham for a brief period, moved back to Caernarvon, and then, once again, to London. Three days later the V-1 "flying bomb" raids started. When the worst was over we moved again to North Wales but came back to London to undergo the siege of V-2 rockets. It wasn't until 1948 that my parents finally made a providential move by leaving the drab austerity of England to return to Canada, where they remained for the next thirty-five years of their lives. They died within a few years of each other at the ages of eighty-nine and ninety-two.

My mother was a large, florid woman who bore an uncanny resemblance, both facially and in mannerisms, to the British character actress Margaret Rutherford. Despite her lengthy sojourns in Canada, she remained quintessentially English, with an intense proprietary interest in the Royal Family. One of my earliest memories is of trailing my parents out of a cinema after having watched a newsreel of the abdication speech of King Edward VIII. My mother thought his behavior "disgraceful" and when my father tried to defend him by mildly pointing out that after all "it was for the woman he loved," my mother stopped in her tracks, threw out her formidable chest, and barked, "That has nothing to do with it! Think of the money we've spent on his *education*!" A product of the Victorian era, she embodied all the middle-class prejudices and snobberies of that period, which imbued her with a fierce determination that I, her only son, would get a good education, so that I would never have to get a job "where I got my hands greasy." This ambition resulted in my always being the least affluent student in a bewildering series of "good" schools. An omnivorous reader, her literary taste was limited by only one stipulation: she only read material that had a "happy ending." This inflexible requirement produced an unusual method of reading a novel: first she would skim the first fifteen pages, then the last ten to make sure there were no "unpleasant surprises," and only then would she settle down to devour the middle of the book. As she grew older her eccentricities became more plentiful. Always a compulsive letter writer, she took to adding afterthoughts on the outside of envelopes. Some of these public postscripts had a chilling import, and I once received an envelope decorated with the bold scrawl, "Turned out he had cancer!" I tore open the envelope to discover this medical diagnosis was of a neighbor's dog. Another memorable "teaser" was the puzzling "Lynn's tart has gone totally bald"—this in reference to my ex-brother-in-law's new wife, who I later discovered had undergone having her head shaved in preparation for surgery.

My father was an attractive, slim man with a gentle, sweet disposition. A gardener by vocation and a mechanic by trade (hence my mother's aversion to greasy hands), he had little formal education, but his lack of intellectual pretensions disguised a dry, sly wit. During the last three years of his life my father lived alone, surrounded by a large assortment of well-tended indoor plants. Whenever I visited him he always bragged about one particular African violet. "Best plant I ever had," he'd say. "Water it twice a week and it blooms all the time." When he died we found out the plant was plastic. At first I was appalled but then realized (or perhaps preferred to believe) that this was typical of my father's sense of humor and, as a writer of comedy, was amused by the expert setup and posthumous payoff.

To the casual observer this perennially youthful man with the kindly, passive demeanor and this rather plain, ambitious, distempered woman with the intensely curious, quick mind must have seemed like an ill-matched couple. The union sometimes puzzled even me but the marriage endured and, always emotionally connected, the two became inseparable towards the end of their lives. This total togetherness made for some peculiar living arrangements. They took to watching different television programs while in the same room. Sitting back-to-back in chairs placed in the middle of the floor, my father would tune into a Western on one TV set, and my mother to Lawrence Welk on another set. The evening's viewing would commence with much shouted-over-the-shoulder instructions to "Turn yours down, Fred," or, "I can't hear mine!" When calling my parents I always let the phone ring about twenty times, knowing that it would take that long before the ringing was heard over the cacophony of galloping horses and bleating saxophones.

Some facts about my parents' marriage were revealed to me in an unusual manner. In 1976 they celebrated (my father said "observed" would be a more accurate word) their sixtieth anniversary. Jill and I flew from Los Angeles to Toronto to give them a party. By then I had written a number of successful television series and had a hit Broadway play, so because of my minor celebrity status a local TV station decided to produce an hour-long interview with my parents. I was not surprised that my mother, always the more vocal of the two, did most of the talking, but what astonished me was that she seemed to have forgotten she was on national television and proceeded to spew forth the most intimate details of her marriage. Asked if she and her husband had ever thought of separating, she replied, "Yes, but then I found out I was pregnant with young Bernard." News to me. At the end of the hour the slightly nonplussed interviewer, trying to end the program on a warm, sentimental note, asked my mother, "Bessie, after sixty years of marriage, if you could do it all over again, would you change anything?" My mother thought for a moment and then said, "Yes, I'd have married a professional man."

My feelings about my mother and father as parents are tinged with ambivalence. Although they were always loving in an understated, undemonstrative way, I regret that they never permitted me, even as an adult, to reveal who I really was to them. This was as much my fault as theirs. Always a facile role player, I too easily slipped into the part of the dutiful, responsible son I believed they preferred. Later, when the roles changed and I became the "parent" to them, that mask was also clamped too firmly in place to permit intimate revelations. Paradoxically, they never tried to influence me in my choice of career or in any of the personal decisions I made in my life, and I believe I reaped the rewards of this benign neglect.

The younger of my two sisters, Shirley, is nine years older than I, and since both my sisters married young, I was raised as an only child. This is one reason why books became important early companions. I used to take books to bed with me. Literally. Every night I would stuff a dozen or so of my favorite novels under the sheets and, after introducing the characters from one book to the characters in another, I would devise stories for this motley cast before happily drifting off to sleep. If this somewhat bizarre habit bothered my parents they rarely verbalized any concern. Occasionally, when my mother was making my bed she'd get a perplexed look on her face and ask, "Aren't you uncomfortable?" but that was as far as it went.

I did not live in the same house for longer than a year until I was married, and because of my parents' wanderlust I attended at least eleven grammar schools. This gypsy-like existence, apart from leaving gaps in my education, obviously played a part in shaping my sensibilities as a writer. Always the "new boy," both extremely shy and gregarious, I evolved a personality of the class wit and carefully honed my skills as a raconteur. This crowd-pleasing ploy, along with a fortunate aptitude for all sports, helped me navigate the shoals of adolescence.

This ability to communicate through comedy and the talent to reshape pain in a comic memory are usually learned early by writers of humor. In my case these means of survival were heavily reinforced by the heady discovery of the ability to produce laughter in others. Laughter was my friend, shared laughter my greatest pleasure, so it is really not so surprising that when I started to write I was drawn to the field of comedy.

I have lived my life to date in Canada, England, and the United States and for a while regretted that this fragmented background deprived me of a specific "regional" voice. I always felt familiar with but not really part of any of these cultures and envied those writers with more identifiable backgrounds, which they could explore in their work. But as I grew older I realized that the peculiar mix of influences in my life had helped me unconsciously evolve a style and vision that, if not unique, was certainly personal.

At the time that my play *Tribute* played Toronto my parents were becoming rather frail, but since they had expressed a desire to see the play, we arranged for a limousine to pick them up and transport them to the theater. There Jill got them settled into their seats next to my sister Brenda, who was assigned the task of making sure that they didn't distract the actors by falling asleep. At the end of the performance I made my way to their side and asked how they liked the play. My mother informed me that they had enjoyed it, but since they had both lost their hearing aids under the seat, they hadn't heard much of the dialogue. She blithely stated that I could "fill them in on that later." She then said, "You know what I really liked the best?" I eagerly asked, "What was that, mum?" She said, "Seeing Eaton's again." Eaton's is a downtown department store they had passed during their limousine ride.

Once I became a writer I was never sure if my parents really understood what I did for a living. After seeing the movie *Same Time, Next Year* my father said, "That Alan Alda sure says some funny things." I told him that I was the one who had written those funny things. "All of them?" he asked. "All of them," I said. He shook his head in amazement. I'm not sure whether he believed me, but it didn't really bother me that my father, a mechanic, was mystified by my work. I am equally baffled when I look at a carburetor.

★ Laughs among the ruins

My own fondness for romantic comedies played out in beautiful drawing rooms grew out of the circumstances of my childhood. I was born in the small town of St. Catharines, near the Canadian side of Niagara Falls, and spent the first four and a half years of my life there and in the even smaller town of Port Dalhousie, where my father operated the local Shell gas station. The Great Depression, along with my mother's nostalgia for England, caused my parents to pull up stakes and, with my two sisters and me in tow, book passage on the *Mauretania*, bound for Liverpool. Our crossing was in December, but the heavy seas and gray skies didn't squelch the beginning of my love of ocean liners, which has persisted to this day. Apart from a pretty playmate named Marigold and my first dog, a mongrel named Laddie, I don't remember much about my early life in Canada (I can hear the reader give a sigh of relief), and my memories of the first few years in England, when my father drove a moving van as a living, are sketchy.

My first recollections are of when I was about seven. We were living in South Croydon, a suburb of London, in a house that was one of a row of attached two-story dwellings, all identical except for different-colored front doors with slated doorsteps, highly polished by competitive housewives, and situated about six feet behind tired-looking privet hedges. Our neighbors were the respectable, typically British working-class people so often depicted in English war films, which glorified them as the "backbone of the Empire." My father was now working as a mechanic in an aircraft factory at Croydon airport, and we were the only family on the street who could afford a car. It was called a Clino and was leather ... on the outside. I'm not making this up, but don't ask me to explain. I do remember going on a summer holiday to Devon that ended with a hair-raising ride home because, for some reason, the car refused to go into reverse.

My mother and father, by the standards of those days, were old parents and my first clear memories of them were when they were in their late forties. My father used to play cricket with me on Sunday picnic outings, but neither of them tried to be "pals." It wasn't something to which English parents aspired and certainly not anything I expected. At that point, friends were much more important in my life. Parents were just there ... they'd always been there ... providing a taken-for-granted security and continuity in a world where there were literally no divorces. This was the backdrop for a mundane life of soccer playing, roller skating to school and the library, devouring books such as the Just William and Biggles series, scrumping apples, being a Cub Scout, skinning knees, playing "conkers" or marbles depending on the season, and generally getting into benign mischief. The ordinary, normal life of a nine-year-old British schoolboy. This all changed one Sunday morning in September 1939.

I can distinctly remember playing with my Dinkie toy cars on the linoleum floor of our living room as my parents listened to Neville Chamberlain's radio announcement that we were formally at war. At the end of his speech, my father, who had spent four years in the trenches in World War I, and mother simply stared at one another, no words adequate. This silence was pierced by the loud wailing of an air-raid siren. Both my sisters, Brenda and Shirley, were at home and we all scrambled down into our Anderson shelter, a structure of corrugated metal sheets that had been hastily assembled in a dirt hole in the garden during the past week. The sirens were a false alarm but helped my parents decide that I should be evacuated out of London the next morning. My feelings were a mixture of trepidation at having to leave my parents and, I have to admit, a tinge of excitement about the adventure in store. That night, when the sirens sounded twice more and I was pulled out of my bed and tumbled into the garden where we all huddled in the damp shelter until the all clear sounded, I simply wanted to be someplace where I could sleep undisturbed through the night.

The next day, wearing the standard schoolboy uniform of short, gray pants, striped cap and blazer, kneesocks that, as usual, sagged in accordion folds around my ankles, and a large, homemade cardboard name tag pinned to my blue raincoat, I joined the hundreds of other evacuees milling around the platform of a railway station. All of us were lugging suitcases, clutching already-grease-stained brown bags of sandwiches packed by our mums, and holding onto containers with the recently government-issued black rubber gas masks inside that would be a permanent part of our dress code for years to come. Fortunately, the only function this grim accessory would serve during the war would be as an aid to schoolboys in creating juicy raspberry noises.

The scene at the station was one of chaos: mothers, some stoic, some damp eyed, smothering their children with hugs; bewildered school teachers wandering around in a daze as they tried to locate their charges; swarms of British soldiers in ill-fitting new khaki uniforms, dragging lethal-in-a-crowd kit bags and looking as disoriented as the children, pushing and cursing as they tried to find their assigned carriages ... all of this added to the pall of uncertainty hanging over the melee. Eventually, we were herded onto a train that, with children hanging out its windows for a last wave good-bye, puffed out of the station, headed for the seaside town of Brighton, some sixty miles away. The choice of Brighton as a place to protect children from air raids was just one of the misguided decisions the authorities made in those early days of the war. It turned out to be right in the path of the incoming German bombers. Luckily, by the time this happened we had all dispersed to other areas.

When we reached Brighton a group of us were driven around for hours to various houses where all but four of us were deposited. By this time, it was dusk and I remember watching the teacher in charge standing under a lamppost, earnestly talking to an elderly woman who kept glancing over at us and shaking her head. Evidently, she had agreed to take in some children, but she wanted girls, not boys. As if this were not enough, wisps of yellow fog were starting to roll in. All the scene needed was a violin. Finally, the woman relented and we were admitted to a house not very different from the one I had just left. Our "foster parents" seemed ancient to our young eyes and, I later learned, were indeed quite elderly. Both were very kind in a no-nonsense sort of way, and we came to call them "Mum" and "Dad." That night, after a supper of cucumber sandwiches, we split up into two bedrooms and I quickly fell into my usual deep sleep.

It may seem surprising that a nine-year-old, taken from a loving family and deposited in a strange household, should so effortlessly take up a new life with no apparent trauma, but there were some factors that might explain it. My two sisters were nine and eleven years older, which meant I was raised as an only child, so suddenly having three other kids my own age to keep me company and share experiences was very appealing. Also, because of the huge influx of children, we were only required to go to school half-days! Can you imagine what a wonderful gift that was for a nine-year-old? Despite the disruptions of those early years I always think of my childhood as being happy. My son recently said to me that he was "programmed for happiness." Maybe it's in the genes. Of course, I missed my parents, but by saving their petrol coupons, they managed to drive down once a month. They also took me home for Christmas, a memorable ride with my father inching the car through a thick, pea soup fog common to England in those days with one of the fathers who was riding with us punctuating the tension every few minutes with, "Coo, good job, you're a good driver." This became a catch phrase in our family.

The important event of that Christmas, though, was that before being driven home to Croydon, I was taken to see my first stage show. At this point my ambitions were the same as any British schoolboy: to become an international cricket or soccer star. However, these boyhood fantasies were expanded when I became fatally stagestruck on the Brighton pier at a performance of the pantomime, *Dick Whittington*. Absolutely enchanted with the music, bright lights, costumes, and charm of the Principal Boy (traditionally, of course, played by a girl … no wonder the British have some gender problems), I passionately wanted to be part of that magical life "up there" on the stage. My love affair with the theater never diminished, and my heart still beats faster when the house lights dim before an opening curtain.

During the nine months I spent in Brighton I met the Tugwells' son, who was later killed in Crete, saw my first naked girl (the Tugwells' ten-year-old granddaughter, Beryl, whom I encountered on the stairs as she was on her way to use the outside lavatory and with whom, of course, I immediately fell in love), and shared adventures with my three roommates.

Our group consisted of an excessively fat boy named Lacey, Norman, a nervous kid with a pronounced facial tic, and Colin, a near-silent lad who endlessly sketched graphic depictions of planes being blown to smithereens in aerial dogfights. A motley crew, but I remember them fondly. Whenever my adult friends have "we were so poor" contests about their upbringing I can always win by asking "Did you have a bathroom?" The Tugwells' house had no bathtub, so every Saturday morning we were sent off to rinse away the week's grime from our gamy small bodies at the public baths. These consisted of numbered cubicles where we were given soap but not the authority or ability to control the flow of water. Sitting in the tub we would yell over the transom "More hot in number four!" or "More cold in number three!" Ingeniously, we would eke out an extra tuppence to buy sweet "gob stoppers" by doubling up in the bath, desperately hoping that we wouldn't get fat Lacey as our partner, not only because he took up most of the tub but because he possessed the talent to fart at will (there's one in every group) and delighted in producing noxious geysers of bubbles in the water.

This was the year dubbed the "phony war" because no major actions took place and my days passed pleasantly enough with only two significant events taking place in my life. In those days every student took an exam called an "eleven-plus," which determined whether he or she would get a scholarship to a grammar school or be streamed into what was basically a trade school. I was considered bright for my age and so was pushed into taking the eleven-plus two years ahead of schedule. I thought I had done okay, but we later were given the news that I did not pass. The other event was that I learned to fight. I was a good soccer player and a fair cricketer, but I never had any desire to put my fists into anyone's face. However, we had a gym teacher who, to stop fights in the playground, came up with the wrong-headed idea that students with a quarrel should announce it and then settle their differences in the boxing ring. This gave the bullies in the class, and there were always two or three, a chance to legitimately beat up on any kid they thought couldn't fight back. I was one of the first kids picked on, with the rather bizarre reason that "he tore my raincoat." The aggressor was bigger than I and I ended up with a closed black eye, but one of my flurry of blows landed squarely on his nose and the blood that spurted out scared the hell out of him. He never bothered me again. This was an important lesson as, subsequently, I attended eleven schools and there was always a bully to deal with before settling into a normal routine. At one school, on my first day, a boy across the classroom caught my eye, pointed to the clock, held up the fingers indicating the minutes left before recess, pointed at me, and pantomimed fists smashing into my face by hitting his own cheeks and pushing his nose sideways. I pragmatically accepted that sometime during the first days at a new school I would end up in a playground scuffle, watched by all the other boys, who would come racing over when they heard the time-honored cries of "Fight! Fight!" I often ended up with a "thick ear," but I learned how to look after myself. This ability, combined with an aptitude for being able to tell a joke, helped me overcome the stigma of always being the new kid on the block.

We also grew very fond of the Tugwells. Eventually, I was taken home because there had been no air raids on London and I never saw them again. After the war I tried to locate them, but addresses lost during the chaotic process of countless moves conspired against a reunion.

About a month after I got home, the war came much closer to home. We heard the sirens, but this time it wasn't a false alarm. My mother and I retreated to the shelter and sat listening to the god-awful noise of the whistling bombs followed by earth-shaking thumps as they landed not too far away. Finally, they stopped, but since the all clear had not sounded, we remained in the shelter. I looked up to see my father framed in the doorway. The sight has remained with me the way certain moments of movies stay etched in our minds. The white coat he wore in his job as a mechanic was covered in blood, his face and black hair were dead white, and he reeked of perfume. He was the only surviving member of the section of factory he worked in at Croydon airport, a bomb blast having blown him under a steel table. The blood was not his own but came from the wounded he had carried to his car and transported to hospital, his hair was filled with white dust, and the smell came from a nearby perfume factory that had also been hit. He was quite deaf for months and, even years later, tiny bits of glass would work their way out of his back. This was the first raid of the Battle of Britain.

The daylight raids continued daily, but somehow, between the attacks, we managed to move to a house my parents had rented a few blocks from Croydon airport, where a Hurricane fighter squadron was based. Our new home was a step up, a stucco semi-detached house with a living room featuring French doors (a sure sign we were now middle class) that opened out onto a large back garden. A graceful staircase led up to three bedrooms. I slept upstairs only once. The first night a bomb blast blew me out of bed and I woke up sprawled at the foot of the stairs. As my mother tried to create some semblance of a home, my father and some of our new neighbors attempted the difficult task of shoveling through the chalky earth in the garden to create a homemade shelter.

Although the Battle of Britain took place during the daylight hours, in the cloudless blue skies of August and September 1941, my parents elected to spend our nights in the makeshift shelter too. We had five bunks and I slept on the top one, with the corrugated iron roof about six inches from my head. I say "slept" because that's exactly what I did, creating a lifelong habit of being able to drop into a deep sleep in any circumstance. Sometimes, when the night bombing was taking place, I would awaken after hours of massive explosions, with neighborhood houses reduced to rubble, and ask "Anything happen last night?" It's a wonder somebody didn't throttle me.

At some time during those years, probably early in the war, my parents decided to evacuate me to Canada to stay with an aunt in Vancouver, and I was duly vaccinated and fitted out with the proper clothes. The journey didn't come to pass because the ship that left before the one on which I was scheduled to sail, and which was also carrying evacuees, was sunk by German torpedoes and my parents opted to keep me at home. I still think this was a good move.

It is true that human beings will become used to anything and that the extraordinary very quickly becomes ordinary. My days started with picking my way through the rubble on my way to school, searching for pieces of bomb shrapnel or fragments of anti-aircraft shells. Once there, the classes seemed less tedious because we were almost certain we would be interrupted by an air raid. If that happened, the entire class would transfer to the concrete school shelters where the lesson would continue, with any lack of concentration forgiven because of the battle sounds outside.

When anybody learns that I went through the London blitz their immediate reaction is that it must have been horrible for me. Well, not really. Anything that disrupts the boring routine of childhood is welcomed by a twelve-year-old. Wartime heightens life and adds the spice of danger, and the possibility of death, paradoxically, makes people seem more alive. In wartime England, class barriers broke down and a spirit of camaraderie brought everyone together. This atmosphere rubbed off on the children, who, with most parents working in factories or enlisted in the armed forces, enjoyed the relaxing of peacetime discipline. It must be remembered, however, that I was fortunate that nobody close to me was killed or injured. Although I was exposed to the destruction of buildings, I was sheltered from actually seeing any of the millions of wartime casualties.

The main deprivation for a child was the diet, and it wasn't until I moved to Canada after the war that I realized bread wasn't supposed to be gray. I recently read that the wartime diet of one egg a month, no sweets, and no butter was the healthiest in the world, but at the time it was difficult to stomach (sometimes literally) and I was grateful for the tins of Spam that a Canadian soldier, who eventually married my sister Brenda, brought to the house. As for the bombing, the only raids that really frightened me were the Buzz Bombs, which you would hear sputtering along before they abruptly cut out—thirty seconds of dead silence while you waited to see if your number was up, an explosion, and strained laughter, as you realized someone other than you had been blown to kingdom come.

Thousands of children had the same wartime experiences, so it's really an oft-told tale. Some forty years later, I was transfixed as I watched John Boorman's film *Hope and Glory*. We are the same age, I believe some of the movie was shot about five miles from where I lived, and almost every event depicted in the film had also occurred in my life. I went to see the film a second time the next day because the similarities were so astonishing.

The aircraft factory where my father worked was relocated to a slate quarry hidden in the mountains of North Wales, out of reach of German bombers. Being wrenched once again from new school friends was made more agreeable by the promise that I would be sleeping in a proper bed. We first lived in the village of Llanberis at the foot of Mount Snowden in a cottage with no electricity or running water, then quickly moved to other primitive houses in other villages. The lack of conveniences must have been hard on my mother, and the only ones who enjoyed this country living were

My mother and father during World War I. Dad was on leave from France.

With my father at his garage in Port Dalhousie on my first birthday.

Me at two years with my dog, Laddie.

Seven years old at Hove, Sussex.

In Waenfaws, North Wales during World War II with our dog, Buck. I was eleven.

As a young actor in Toronto, circa 1952.

Jill, as a young actress at the start of her career in television.

My mother and father on our wedding day, July 25, 1953.

Very early days in summer stock at Allanburg, near Niagara Falls. The play was *The Family Upstairs* and I'm the one with the cushion in my stomach and the white shoe polish in my hair.

Dad, Jill, and me, shortly after Jill and I were married.

My very first cheque for a television script called *The Prizewinner,* 1957.

The theater where I lost twenty-five pounds and my hair turned gray. It was all very character building.

The most inefficient steward in aviation history.

Mum and our daughter Laurie in 1958.

Taken right after our arrival in California. Do you wonder why we liked it?

The year we arrived in Los Angeles and everyone went blond.

Chris, not long before he started beating me.

Oh well, they can't *all* be winners.

My good friend E. W. Swackhamer, known to all as "Swack," and Jerry Davis, who helped inspire *Tribute* and brightened my days.

Carl Reiner, me, Brenda Vacarro, and Jose Ferrer during shooting of the pilot film for *Everything Money Can't Buy* in San Francisco, 1974.

our wonderful family dog, Buck, who hadn't been too crazy about the bombing either, and me.

My mother, to her everlasting credit, fought her way through a morass of wartime red tape to get the actual results of the eleven-plus exam I had taken and learned that I had failed to pass by only four marks. This near miss and my young age earned me a scholarship to Caernarvon Grammar School, where I enjoyed my only experience with a coeducational student body (and sometimes bodies) of my school days. Most of the students were Welsh and would switch from English to Welsh and back with astounding facility. Although I never spoke Welsh I must have absorbed some of the language because, years later, while watching a television production of *The Corn Is Green* I automatically found myself translating the Welsh dialogue into English for Jill.

Most of the regular school staff were serving in the armed forces, so elderly teachers were dragged out of retirement and I was exposed to a series of wonderfully eccentric instructors. One was a heavyset woman given to wearing thick tweed suits under her tattered gown. She was easily identified by her habit of always carrying a roll of toilet paper with her. Upon entering a classroom, she would rip off portions of paper and vigorously polish the chair she was about to sit on in order to remove any chalk dust that might sully her Harris tweed skirt. I once spotted her on a bus and she cleaned that seat too. Our Latin teacher was so deaf that when a pupil was asked to stand and conjugate verbs he would silently move his lips while the boy next to him read out loud from the textbook. An art teacher, Mr. Smoothie, wore suede shoes but no socks, green corduroy trousers, a grubby yellow turtleneck sweater, and sported the longest cigarette holder I have ever seen, which he used as a pointer, to scratch his head, and even to clean his ears.

I suppose that everyone has one memorable teacher who has affected their lives. Mine was an English master named Mr. MacLeod, who would often start the class by simply opening a book and reading in a mellifluous voice, immediately drawing us into the fascinating world of such stories as *Treasure Island* and *A Tale of Two Cities*. Just as he reached an exciting turn of the plot he would snap the book shut and say, "The book can be procured at the public library." We couldn't wait to get there.

We moved into a flat in the town of Caernarvon, but then, as a result of my mother's never-ending search for "something better," we moved again ... and again ... and again. Some thirty years later when I revisited Caernarvon with my wife and children, as we were being driven through the town, I would point and say, "I lived there," "And I lived there," and "I lived there," etc. Finally my daughter said, "My God, how long were you in this town?" I said, "A year." Actually, I was there for two years, as I attended the same school twice, but why spoil a good joke with facts.

My parents always took me to the movies once a week ... in those days you didn't go to see a specific film, you just "went to the movies" ... and you didn't even go at the beginning of the film but wandered in anytime during the double bill and left when the story indicated that "this is where we came in." My sister Brenda and her Canadian fiancé also took me at least once a week, and a variety of after school and weekend jobs, such as delivering groceries on a heavy, fat tired bike, earned me the money to pay for yet another show myself. This movie-going habit became ingrained, staying with me all through my nomadic war years, influencing and shaping my tastes. I liked the musicals and romantic comedies best. They were the ones that provided the most wonderful escape into a magical world where everyone was attractive, drove fancy cars, and, if they weren't singing and dancing their hearts out, said smart, sophisticated bon mots ... all of this played out in glorious technicolor in direct contrast to the wartime drabness around us. Is it any wonder I ended up writing romantic comedies?

The theater didn't play a major part in my life until the end of the war, when I was back in Croydon and there were two weekly repertory companies, the Croydon Grand and the Penge Rep., that could be reached by a short bus ride. Usually seeing two plays a week, plus haunting the Croydon Empire, a music hall theater featuring all the comedy and musical greats of that era, I happily absorbed a steady diet of Noël Coward, Somerset Maugham, Daphne du Maurier, Frederick Lonsdale, and Emlyn Williams and laughed myself silly at the farces of Ben Levy and Philip King. This early inclination for the popular rather than the profound has remained with me and, although my theater-going tastes are quite eclectic, I still believe the primary function of the theater is to entertain.

When I graduated from grammar school I had not clearly defined what I wanted from life, but I quickly realized what I did not want. One morning on my daily commute to the London Stock Exchange where I had taken a fill-in job as a messenger, I glanced back along London Bridge and saw hundreds of bowler-topped men, tightly rolled umbrellas in hand, marching towards their jobs of doing "something in the city." At that moment (as a dramatist I tend to see life as a series of blinding epiphanies) I knew with absolute certainty that the suburban businessman's life was not for me.

My first active involvement with the theater came about through a friend named David Prockter. We had met when we were twelve and were students at John Ruskin Grammar School. A mathematics teacher had chalked an equation on the blackboard and turned to the class and asked, "Now, what's that?" Getting no reply, he barked, "Now, don't be shy. If you think it's an equation, say so. If you think it's a laundry bill, say so. If you think it's an elephant, say so." David raised his hand. "Sir, I think it's an elephant." We are friends to this day.

David asked me to accompany him to an amateur theater group in Croydon, where we could "meet girls." We met girls, in my case one in particular named Wendy, and I was cast in the first produced play of Noël Coward called *I'll Leave It to You*. On opening night, when I walked onto the stage, I was gradually suffused with a curious sense of serenity. Insecure, somewhat uncomfortable with my real-life persona, I felt more at ease in the classic country-house living room than in any place I had ever been. I was destined to appear in many similar sets during my career as an actor. Many years later, I bought a house because I immediately felt completely at home in the living room. It wasn't until some weeks had passed before I realized my feeling of familiarity was because the beamed ceilings, French doors, and brick fireplace of the room mirrored so many of the sets in which I had acted.

My initial attempt at writing occurred during this period, when David and I cowrote a boardinghouse farce called *Vicious Circle*, which unabashedly mimicked the form, but not the expertise, of the Whitehall farces we had been avidly attending. I had absolutely no idea if it showed any promise of talent or not; all I remember is that, at the time, we thought it was brilliant.

However, any realization of dreams of an immediate career in the professional theater was delayed by my parents' decision to immigrate again to Canada. For me to stay in England would mean that I would have to serve two years in the army, which, given my loathing for any kind of institutional authority, would have been a horrendous experience. I bid a painful good-bye to Wendy and my close-knit band of friends and boarded the *Aquatania*, bound for the country of my birth.

★ Enter the leading lady

A recent calculation made me realize that the second time my parents immigrated to Canada my father was fifty-six. Fifty-six, with almost no money and no job. Just pluck and luck. They moved back to St. Catharines, about eighty miles from Toronto, where he managed to get a job at the General Motors plant. He stayed there until he was retired ten years later (he'd lied about his age by a year), still with no money. His luck held because by then, miraculously, I had made enough money to put a down payment on a small house in Toronto for them, where they lived out their long retirement.

I stayed in Toronto and, at first, the unaccustomed peacetime luxuries of ice cream, butter, sugar, and eggs were exciting, but the novelty of these creature comforts quickly paled beside the fact that, for the first and perhaps only time in my life, I was desperately lonely. In those pre-Beatles times it was unfashionable in Canada to be English, and I was very, very English, with longish, heavily brilliantined hair and a penchant for purple corduroy jackets and, I have to admit, imitation silk ascots. This improbable garb, more suited to a seedy, over-the-hill provincial rep actor than an eighteen-year-old, made it difficult to win friends among my crew-cut, hockey-loving contemporaries. I landed a job working as a Clerk-Grade II for the Customs and Excise Department in a large, gray building in Toronto, where I spent my days in a small wire cage frantically stamping thousands of mysterious documents that were shoveled at me through a small aperture. My coworkers, for the most part, were civil servants who seemed to spend an inordinate amount of time discussing the government pensions that would be paid them some thirty-five years in the future. During the next eighteen months I wrote weekly mournful letters to my friends in England, saw countless movies, attended a series of dismal dances at the YMCA in the almost always unsuccessful quest for female companionship, and joined a soccer club of expatriate Britons. This last activity resulted in my leg being broken in three places, which meant I was encased in a toe-to-hip plaster cast for four boiling-hot summer months. The picture I created standing on one foot in my cage, crutches by my side, stamping the still-mysterious documents, must have been truly Dickensian. Of course, at eighteen and optimistic by nature, I didn't consciously acknowledge that I was lonely, and it was only some time later, when someone pointed out that my first seven television plays were all about loneliness, that I realized how traumatic this period had been. Not surprisingly, my subsequent plays were all about friendship. My salvation, not for the first or last time, was the theater.

In 1950, homegrown theater in Canada was almost nonexistent and, apart from isolated Toronto productions of plays cast primarily with radio actors who possessed beautiful speaking voices but no discernible stage technique, the only theatrical opportunities were provided by a handful of summer-stock companies. One of the pioneers of this movement was an ex-high-school English teacher named Jack Blacklock, who had started a summer-stock company in Midland, Ontario, and was now planning a season of six productions in the Museum Theatre of the University of Toronto. I answered his newspaper ad for actors and it was here that I first met my future wife, Jill Foster, who later became one of Canada's more successful actresses.

The night I met her she was wearing a belted blue raincoat and a navy beret clamped over her blond hair, topping a pair of amazing blue eyes. She also possessed a low, melodious voice that was very easy on the ears. As you can see, I hardly noticed her at all. The only thing I wasn't crazy about was her name, Florence Hancock, but, as was the custom with actors in those days, she soon changed it to the more theatrical Jill Foster. My full name is Bernard Slade Newbound and I also changed it by dropping the surname ... something I've often regretted as the name Newbound is unique. However, at the time I didn't think it would look good up in lights!

Jill was born and raised in Toronto in a family that consisted of three older brothers and one younger sister. She was educated in Catholic schools and, perhaps because she was a good student, was regularly asked by the nuns if she had "got the call yet?" She hadn't, at least not from the church, but the theater was beginning to send out its siren song. When I first met her she was working as a secretary in a Toronto stockbroker's office, but a chance elocution lesson had fanned her enthusiasm for the theater and she had answered the same ad that I had.

When we went out for coffee that night with the rest of the group I can't say that we were hit by a blinding passion. I can't even say that she was "my type" ... at nineteen I didn't have a "type" ... it was more a case of gender. Anyway, any thoughts of romance were unrealistic as Jill was almost engaged to some stockbroker-type who I claimed looked old enough to be her father, and I was too poor to date, let alone marry. However, there was some attraction ... I thought she was pretty (still do) and she laughed at my jokes. This last asset is highly prized by comedy writers and is often the glue that keeps a relationship together. Eventually, fate would throw us together and give romance a chance to bloom, but that was later.

I was first cast as a drunken old man in the Anita Loos play *Happy Birthday* and after the performance was asked to join the summer company. I promptly quit my job at Customs and reported to the Niagara Barn Players in a small village called Allenburg, located between Niagara Falls and my birthplace, St. Catharines, to begin a ten-year career as a professional actor. After pitching in to convert a barn into a rustic 350-seat (actually, bench) theater, we embarked on a season of sixteen productions, playing, in those pretelevision times, to absolutely packed, enthusiastic houses.

Jack Blacklock was an unusual character. Unusual and very, very weird. An oddly proportioned man, he had a very large head, which gave rise to his oft-uttered theory that "all great actors have large heads." Actually, he was an excruciatingly bad actor who would miscast himself in leading roles and inflict on audiences performances that had to be seen to be disbelieved. As a director his instruction was always the same: "Louder, faster, funnier." To be fair, with only five days of rehearsal for each play, this wasn't such a bad note. However, his habit of standing in the wings and giving speed-up signals to the actors on stage was extremely unnerving. But it was his everyday behavior that was most bizarre and terrified the hell out of the company. We could always foretell his frequent fits of rage because he was afflicted with a severe body tic that, when he was provoked, would cause his large frame to go into spasmodic tremors. These rages would prompt him to fire actors for various infractions—usually for not being loud, fast, or funny enough. His method of letting people go was unique. We had communal dressing rooms, and the hapless actor selected for dismissal would come offstage to find a message scrawled in greasepaint across his mirror that read: "You're fired!!" Blacklock was given to addressing the cast after performances with long, irrational speeches delivered from the stage, illuminated by only the footlights (yes, we had them in those days), which gave his face a maniacal, macabre look. He owned a Chihuahua, improbably named Bomber, who, during a performance of *Peg o' My Heart*, was discovered copulating backstage with a large spaniel who was appearing in the play. No amount of water poured on the two dogs could separate them until they had fully consummated their friendship. This meant that an actress had to make her entrance carrying a satisfied but soaking-wet cocker spaniel in her arms. That night all the cast was assembled in the front row of the theater except for the wretched apprentice responsible for the dogs. She was trapped up on stage. In the middle of Blacklock's tirade, delivered as he paced back and forth, this poor girl keeled over in a dead faint. Nobody moved—except for Blacklock, who, without missing a beat, stepped over her prone body as he kept on pacing and shouting. Some weeks later the spaniel gave birth to two very peculiar-looking puppies.

Another scene that has stayed with me, and I'm sure anybody else who witnessed it, took place when we were doing *Uncle Tom's Cabin* with Jack, for once perfectly cast, playing Simon LeGree. At the end of the performance, after our curtain calls, Jack stepped forward to make his usual speech exhorting the audience to tell their friends about the show. Unfortunately, a nervous apprentice named Paul Humbert was working the heavy, canvas drop curtain. He made the ghastly mistake of letting it descend squarely on Jack's head, knocking him to the ground. Jack, in his Simon LeGree costume, rushed into the wings and started to verbally assault the poor boy and beat him with his slave owner's whip. Terrified, Humbert escaped to the front of the house and the audience was treated to the spectacle of Simon LeGree brandishing his whip, chasing a young man down the center aisle and out into the parking lot. We never saw poor Humbert again. This was the sort of experience that binds a company together.

However, it should be said that Jack did have an enormous passion for the theater and, in a country where talk is more prevalent than action, did something about it, giving dozens of actors a chance to "learn on the job" by being on a stage night after night in hundreds of plays.

The plays presented were all chosen for their popular appeal and, over the years, the ones in which I appeared were a very mixed bag. They included *Tobacco Road*, *The Philadelphia Story*, *The Old Soak*, *The Man Who Came to Dinner*, *Ramshackle Inn*, *Come Back Little Sheba*, *Life with Father*, *The Hasty Heart*, *The Vinegar Tree*, *The Curious Savage*, *Years Ago*, *Separate Rooms*, *Night Must Fall*, *Kiss and Tell*, *Harvey*, *My Sister Eileen*, *Meet the Wife*, *The Two Mrs. Carrols*, *The Late Christopher Bean*, and many, many more. Some I barely remember and sometimes I ask a friend, who was around during those years, three questions, "Was I ever in such and such?" "What did I play?" and "Was I any good?"

The operation was so successful that Jack was approached to move the company to another location, where a new theater would be built to his specifications. True to his idiosyncratic nature, he reversed the conventional summer-stock tradition of turning a barn into a theater by building a theater to look like a barn! He subsequently had a nervous breakdown but recovered and lived well into his eighties.

Although only twenty years old, I had a face that took well to character makeup, which helped win me a series of juicy father roles, and my constant companion was a bottle of white shoe polish. This not only grayed my hair but made it so stiff that a ride in an open convertible didn't leave a strand out of place.

One of my more memorable reviews said that my performance as Ed Devery in *Born Yesterday* was "mostly concentrated upon hair treatment." This carping did not disturb me at all. Young, single, and blessed with an almost photographic memory, which relieved me from the drudgery of studying lines, I was being paid to perform every night in the company of kindred spirits, and I felt at home again. Nostalgia for one's youth is not uncommon, of course, but what is rather unusual is that even at the time I sensed that this was about as good as it gets.

It was during these salad days in the early fifties that I first encountered Elwy Yost. An ebullient man, he has never lost his enthusiastic approach to life. Later, during a brief stint reviewing films for the *Toronto Star*, he was known as the "Will Rogers of critics" because he "never met a movie he didn't like." Although only twenty-six when we met, he sported a mustache and had already lost most of his hair, which allowed him to play Sheridan Whiteside in *The Man Who Came to Dinner* without having to age himself with makeup. There was a beneficial side to his unusually mature appearance: some fifty years later he looks exactly the same as he did on the day we met.

Over the next decade our mutual passion for books and films fueled our long-standing friendship even though Elwy drifted out of show business and, after a brief spell as a business executive, became a high-school teacher in Toronto. Some years later I devised a TV game show for the Canadian Broadcasting Corporation called *Live a Borrowed Life* and, since they said they were looking for larger-than-life panelists rather than the incredibly dull, bland people they usually hired, I suggested they audition Elwy. He got the job and soon became very well known in Canada. His fame increased when he was hired by the educational channel in Ontario and became the always genial host and interviewer on the popular program, *Saturday Night at the Movies*.

If Elwy has a fault, if indeed it is a fault, it is his intense desire to please ... everyone. One day his usually favorable mail included a letter from a viewer who was critical of something he had said.

This really bothered Elwy and became like a boil in his armpit, partly because he had taken to always carrying the letter in the inside pocket of his jacket. From time to time he would take it out, reread it, and sadly shake his head, a man misunderstood. About a year later, while driving to his summer cottage, he realized that the letter came from a very small village only a few miles out of his way. He drove to the village, he knocked on the door, and when an absolutely flabbergasted woman answered, he brandished the letter and said, "Now, Madam, about your letter ..." Of course, the woman was speechless ... possibly believing that this was one celebrity who answered all his mail personally ... but managed to find enough words to invite him in for tea, where Elwy resolved all their difficulties and left behind a satisfied fan.

Once while in England, Elwy decided to buy a car. Now, he is about as ignorant about cars as one can be, but a small, open, gleaming red car in a showroom window caught his fancy. In he trotted to try and ask knowledgeable questions of the salesman. The price certainly seemed reasonable, but not wanting to appear a mechanical moron he said, "Well, I suppose I should look at the engine." The salesman said, "The what?" Elwy said, "The engine. You know, the thing that makes it run." The salesman wordlessly pointed. Elwy peered into the car and saw two pedals below the dashboard. It was a toy car. He told me he was tempted to ask if he could take it out on the road for a spin.

Elwy has two sons, Graham and Christopher, and his passion for films caused him to take them to see *Psycho* when the boys were only four and six. I was appalled that he would expose them to this sort of suspense. "Nonsense," he said, "they loved it ... especially Graham." Well, he must have because years later Graham sold his first screenplay. The name of the movie? *Speed*! By the way, I only stopped being frightened by *Psycho* when Tony Perkins told me he wasn't even on the set when they filmed the famous shower sequence. He also gave me a tip: turn the music down while watching it and the film will seem almost benign.

At the end of the summer the company disbanded and I talked my way into a position as a credit manager with a large manufacturer, a job for which I was entirely unsuited. The tedium was relieved by a tour of one-night stands of Kaufman and Hart's *You Can't Take It with You*, in which I played the black servant Donald, a role that involved blacking both my face and legs. One night, having arrived home at 4 A.M., I was too exhausted to take a bath and, still unwashed, straggled in to work the next morning to conduct an interview with a client. Five minutes into the session I noticed the man staring at my leg with an incredulous expression. I glanced down and saw that my raised pant cuff was revealing a portion of shin that was completely black. I didn't even try to offer an explanation (I couldn't think of one that would suffice) but casually pulled my pant leg down. A few awkward minutes later the man excused himself and sidled out of the office, probably convinced that he had been dealing with someone who was black from the waist down.

In the spring I quit my job and rejoined the Niagara Barn Players, starting a pattern that would continue over the next few years of theater work interspersed with a wide variety of "civilian" jobs that even included a stint as a flight attendant on Air Canada, where I gained some notoriety among my fellow stewards by a habit of taking off my jacket, donning sunglasses, and sitting among the passengers.

This last job came about when, after a lover's spat with Jill, I applied for the position, having somehow convinced myself that it was a dramatic gesture equivalent to joining the Foreign Legion. I believed that I would have adventures in all the glamorous capitals of the world and looked forward to flying to London, Paris, Rome, etc. They put me on the Toronto-Winnipeg run.

I had never flown before I took the job, but after a six-week training course in Montreal I quickly became familiar with working on the pre-jet DC-4s. However, I had never taken a night flight. One evening, at dusk, we were on the Toronto runway about to take off when I glanced out the window and saw a blue flame coming out of one of the engines. Now, in our training, we had been taught that in an emergency we should reassure the passengers by doing something completely normal, like handing out magazines from left to right. I did not do this but, in a complete panic, opted to race down the aisle to the door leading to the cockpit, which had a combination lock. When I couldn't remember the combination I was reduced to frantically banging on the door, but evidently the flight crew couldn't hear me over the noise of the engines. Wild-eyed, I raced back to the galley to pick up the intercom. Out of the corner of my eye I could see the passengers, many first-time fliers, showing their concern at the actions of the demented steward, but I didn't care—I had to save us all. I could hear the engines roaring preparatory to takeoff as the captain came on the intercom. "What is it?" he said. "Captain, your engine's on fire!" I said. "Which one?" he said. I peered out of the galley windows to now see four blue flames and said, "All of them!" There were a few moments of silence I can only describe as the sort of pause Bob Newhart used to take in his old telephone routines, and then he said, in his best *Right Stuff* captain voice, "Why don't you sit down? I'll come back and explain later." Aware that by now the passengers were really upset, I assumed an attitude of nonchalance as I sauntered back to my seat. I might even have whistled.

My schedule was to work a flight from Toronto to Montreal, returning immediately to Toronto and then heading for Winnipeg, where the crew would stay overnight before returning to Toronto the next day. The night in Winnipeg was always spent at the Fort Garry Hotel, a traditional, imposing establishment built largely to service railway passengers. Years later, when my second play was being produced at the Manitoba Theatre Centre, I stayed at the same hotel. There was a huge billboard in the lobby that read: World Premiere—Bernard Slade's *A Very Close Family*. One day, dressed in a blue blazer and gray pants, I was standing, admiring the sign and enjoying the fact that, once a lowly flight attendant, I had returned as a playwright with his name, if not in lights, at least up in paint. My reverie was interrupted by a man checking into the hotel who came through the lobby and handed me his suitcase. Brushing aside my protests with "Don't worry, I'll give you your tip later," he sailed on to the front desk. I had no choice but to follow him with his suitcase. I was tempted to point out that the name on the billboard was mine, but I only managed, "Look, I'm not the bellboy." Unfazed, he said, "You *look* like the bellboy."

This was not the only time that I got myself into uncomfortable situations by not speaking up. Some years ago, I was driving in an open convertible along Sunset Boulevard on my way home from the studio. These were the days when people actually picked up hitchhikers and when I came to a red light I was accosted by one. I was very tired and just didn't feel like company, so I said, "Sorry, I'm turning off." The man said, "Where are you going?" I quickly made up a destination about ten miles away. "I'm going to Pico and La Cienega," I said. "Great!" he said and got into the car. "That's exactly where I'm going!" I then proceeded to drive him ten miles out of my way.

During this period of playing in repertory I appeared in about one hundred and fifty plays. I believe this was the best training I received in preparation for my future career as a dramatist. Acting in plays by such writers as Philip Barry, John Van Druten, S. N. Behrman, Noël Coward, Kaufman and Hart, Bernard Shaw, Oscar Wilde, F. Hugh Herbert, and George Kelly, I subconsciously absorbed structure, the mathematics of comedy, the intricacies of characterization, and, perhaps most important of all, the value of an emotional subtext to every scene. In later years, I was certainly capable of writing a flawed scene or even one that didn't belong in the play, but I don't believe I have ever written a scene that couldn't be *played*. It would seem that, being an actor, even a bad one, is a helpful stepping-stone to becoming a dramatist.

By this time television was flickering on all over Canada and Jill had landed a role on a weekly variety show. Our combined incomes made it possible for us to marry, and on July 25, 1953, our wedding took place. It was one of my better decisions.

I suppose that most married couples have tried to trace the steps that brought them together, and the subject has been explored in many films, notably in one of my favorite movies, *But Now My Love*. Although a romantic by nature, I have never really believed that there is only one person in the world who can fulfill one's dreams. However, there were some odd twists and coincidences that brought Jill and me together. We were born a week apart in the same year ... she in Toronto, I in St. Catharines, about eighty miles away. When I was four I left Canada for England, which would seem to preclude our ever meeting. But then, in 1948, I returned and the theater brought us together. Jill's family were violently opposed to our romance, not only because I was an out-of-work actor but also because they had absolutely no interest in the arts ... years later, when we would fly back to Los Angeles after visiting our parents, we would convince each other that we were adopted.

One further event in our lives that, if it had gone a different way, could probably have severed our relationship was that we were both hired to work in a theater in Kingston, but then, at the last moment, I was offered a job in the much more exotic place of Bermuda. I jumped at the chance, but Drew Thompson, who ran the International Players, wouldn't let me out of my contract, so Jill and I boarded a train for Kingston. It was there, amid the hurly-burly of weekly repertory and exposed to the worst aspects of each other but willing to overlook them, that we realized that this wasn't going to be just a summer romance. The company was unique in that it was a "pay what you like" theater, with Arthur Sullivan, the co-producer, stepping in front of the curtain between the acts and beseeching the audience to give generously when the hat was passed around. Our salaries were thirty dollars a week, and after we were paid in small bills and silver we would clank up the street to the local restaurant to stuff ourselves with spaghetti. We were deliriously happy.

The next season Jill and I were in the first blush of falling in love, and I have a vivid memory of us gazing soulfully into each other's eyes as we sat backstage. Not an unusual occurrence between two young people in love, but this picture had a new "wrinkle" because I was made up to look like a rural hayseed with a droopy mustache and unshaven cheeks (one of my Percy Kilbride roles) while Jill had frizzy gray hair and a face marred by deep age lines in her role as an old farm woman. And we still found each other attractive! No wonder the marriage endured.

To this day, a balmy eastern summer night will always transport me back to that carefree period of my life. So will certain pieces of music, like Offenbach's "Gaity Parisienne," which was played to put the audience in a cheerful mood before the opening curtain of a comedy. The smell of greasepaint, now rarely used, the sound of chirping crickets, or a gentle breeze coming off a lake will also quickly conjure up that magical period. Still a nice place to visit, and I wish a similar experience for all young actors.

We have been married for forty-six years and are often asked what is the secret of our marriage. My answer is, "I really don't know." It's true that, to this date, we have led an absolutely charmed life, with no major illnesses, two children of whom we're very proud, and no money worries. But I believe the major reason, apart from blind luck and the fact that we share the same values that we mostly absorbed early in life from nineteenth-century literature, is that we have had a chance to grow, both separately and together.

Jill was a very successful television actress and variety performer in Canada, which, had I not turned to writing, might have created some difficulties. Fortunately, the subject never really came up. She and I had different attitudes about acting. Basically, I liked performing, especially the curtain calls, and disliked the drudgery of rehearsals, while she loved using the rehearsal time to develop the character she was playing. While I was enamored with what my friend Carole Cook calls the "glitter and tits" of show business, Jill was not so easily seduced. Given this attitude, it is not surprising that when we moved to LA and she was only hired to play smaller parts on TV series, she decided to quit acting and go back to school. At thirty-eight, possessing only a high-school diploma, she enrolled as a freshman in UCLA and, over the years, got her BA, her MA, and eventually a degree in Family Counseling. Although never totally convinced that psychotherapy (I call it the "disturbed sciences") was everything it's cracked up to be, she was alarmed when we bought a place in New York. "What am I going to tell my patients?" she said. I said, "Tell them they're cured."

Jill possesses many talents. She's a wonderful cook, a great hostess, and a first-class decorator who can put a house together in a few days, and I have been the benefactor of these attributes. But if I had to pick the most important factors in our relationship, they would be our common sensibility and senses of humor. It's not easy to find someone with whom you can laugh *and* cry.

Shortly after we were married we came up with what we thought was a brilliant idea: we would open our own theater and become very, very rich. I formed a partnership with an American actor named Warren Erhardt and contracted to take over the now available Niagara Barn Theatre in Vineland, located about halfway between Niagara Falls and the city of Hamilton. We rechristened it the Garden Centre Theatre, then hired a company of about sixteen actors, who would all reside in a large boardinghouse near the theater. We had youth, vitality, and fifteen hundred dollars. How could we possibly fail?

Part of our capital was used to buy a vintage British car called the Mayflower, which had been manufactured (and promptly discontinued) by Triumph some years earlier. When the car was delivered both Warren and I went to climb into the passenger seat. "I don't drive," he explained. "Neither do I," I said. Only slightly daunted, I took a three-day driving course, which effectively saddled me with all the chores of arranging to borrow furniture for the sets from local merchants, hauling the props, dropping off the newspaper advertising in the surrounding towns, and even driving the ushers home every night. We did not consider our meager capital a drawback, as our optimistic plan was to make small deposits on all the equipment we needed and then pay it off in six weeks, after we had raked in the receipts from the full houses we expected. The contract with the theater owner stipulated that we begin our season on April 5. Our summer theater opened in a blinding snowstorm. Six weeks and six plays later, we were fifteen thousand dollars in debt. This figure simply numbed our brains: at twenty-four years old we couldn't even conceive of such an amount. My co-producer threatened to depart for the States ("They can't touch me there") and made the helpful suggestion that I declare bankruptcy. But we persevered and the season progressed, with Jill cooking for the actors, me doing a variety of chores, which included cleaning the latrines, and both of us playing a series of large, dull supporting roles. We remedied this last situation by starring in the two-character play *The Fourposter* but naively scheduled it in the middle of the season and so had to financially carry a full company of actors.

Although the twenty-five-week season had some joyful times— after all, we were all very young and resilient, with our senses of humor still intact—the constant worrying about whether we would have enough money to make the payroll and pay for the advertising clouded the summer days. Of course, the main change from the previous seasons when the theater had attracted sell-out audiences was the advent of television, still a novelty and very seductive. I remember each night, after applying my makeup, I would peer out of the dressing-room window into the field that served as a parking lot to count the number of cars, which would tell us what size audience we would have for the show that night. It was only completely filled on Saturday nights, but we were ever hopeful.

This unrelenting pressure probably triggered some odd behavior. One moonlit night, at about 1 A.M., Jill and I were standing on the shallow pebble beach near the theater, gazing out over calm Lake Ontario, enjoying a brief respite from our worries. Then, suddenly Jill said, "Let's go in!" I said, "We don't have any swimsuits." She said, "We don't need any. There's nobody around." Then somewhat surprisingly, since she was a fairly conservative, modest young woman, she slipped out of her clothes and said, "Come on!" I hesitated and said, "No, I'll be the lookout." I watched as she waded out about thirty yards into the black water, until it was up to her waist, and stood looking up at the stars and the fitful moon. I abruptly changed my mind, shucked off my clothes, and silently moved out to join her. "Silently" is the key word here as any noises I might have made were covered by the slight breeze that had sprung up. A few feet behind her I casually said, "You know, you could be arrested for ..." I never did finish the sentence as, with a terrified yelp, she shot out of the water like a Polaris missile. When she reentered the water and realized it was only me, she fell into my arms and our laughter built far out of proportion to what the situation warranted. When it subsided, we looked at each other with the thought, "Are we cracking up?"

The actual performing was the least of our problems, and even though we were presenting a different play every week with only six days' rehearsal, we blithely sailed through such difficult plays as *A Streetcar Named Desire*, and sophisticated comedies like *The Philadelphia Story*.

The Philadelphia Story, by Philip Barry, is one of my favorite romantic comedies and I had considered myself fortunate in being cast in two different productions, both in summer stock. Many years later, when I was working at Screen Gems Studios in Hollywood, I came home from lunch one day to find Cary Grant sitting in my office. Now, I had long ago stopped being overwhelmed by meeting movie actors, but seeing probably the greatest film light-comedian of the twentieth century skimming through *Daily Variety* at my desk did make me wonder what in the world he was doing there. It turned out that my secretary had once been his assistant and he had dropped by to see her. We had a nice, relaxed chat and as the afternoon wore on the conversation turned to the film version of *The Philadelphia Story,* and I had the temerity to tell him that I had once played C. K. Dexter-Haven, the role he had played in the movie. Both of us were huge fans of Jimmy Stewart, who had played the other male lead in the film, and he reminded me of the drunk scene between the two of them in the film, in which Stewart had chosen to play the drunkenness in a brilliant, unique way. No slurring of words, no clichéd, obvious tricks usually employed when playing a man who has imbibed too much. No, Mr. Stewart had opted to play the scene VERY SLOWLY and VERY LOUDLY. Absolutely original, believable, and very funny. Cary Grant said that the next time I saw the scene I should look at a shot of him because Stewart had not rehearsed the scene this way, and the look of astonished admiration on Grant's face was not acting. I enjoyed my afternoon with Cary Grant, but, as a rule, I've found it is not a good idea to meet one's heroes, especially if they are movie actors, because they can rarely live up to the characters they portray on the screen. If you want to enjoy some witty repartee, invite the writer to dinner ... and even then you'll probably be disappointed because most writers need a few hours to come up with scintillating ad-libs.

I've worked with a number of major stars and although I've genuinely liked and respected some, like Jack Lemmon and Melvyn Douglas and Mia Farrow, it's hard to sustain a close relationship with a movie actor for the simple reason that they are never home. Most films today are shot on location, many in far-flung countries, which makes it difficult to get together for potluck suppers. British actors, who usually also work in the theater, tend to stay put more and we have forged strong friendships with Pauline Collins, who became world-famous playing Shirley Valentine, and her husband John Alderton, who is well known in Britain partly because of his appearances on *Upstairs, Downstairs* and his long television career. It's easier to be out in public with British "names" because the public there are usually too polite to intrude. Mia Farrow has a novel way of responding to people who ask, "Are you Mia Farrow?" She simply says "No."

When one has been in show business for a while one does tend to become blasé about celebrities, with the possible exception of actors who were stars when one was growing up and sitting in darkened cinemas, watching these larger-than-life creatures. I have a friend who worked at MGM during its heyday and I once expressed my astonishment that he had dated the likes of Lana Turner and Ava Gardner. He said, "You don't understand. To us, they were just the girls on the block." Not my block. Anyway, one night Jill and I were invited to Jack and Felicia Lemmon's house, to what we assumed would be a small gathering, and since Jack and Felicia tended to hang out with old friends rather than above-the-title people, we didn't bother to dress up, believing it would be a casual, "at home" evening. When I walked into the living room the first person I saw was Gregory Peck. The second was Fred Astaire, and, as my eyes took in the rest of the room, I noticed Billy Wilder, Walter Matthau, and almost every star from my youth. A helicopter landed on the lawn outside and Frank Sinatra entered. When introduced to Jill, he fixed her with his famous blue eyes and said, "You have a very talented husband." Made her day. I don't know how he could possibly have known I was talented, but I was a tad impressed too.

Perhaps the actor I enjoyed meeting the most was Sir John Mills, not only because I had always admired his work but also because, when I was growing up in England, he was the quintessential hero of British films such as *In Which We Serve*, *Hobson's Choice*, and *Great Expectations*. When I met him he was a sweet, rather frail man of ninety, but, despite the fact that he was almost totally blind and deaf, he was completely charming, with an astounding knowledge of the careers of everyone in the room. The consummate actor, he was still doing a one-man show in Britain, which he managed to pull off with the aid of thick white paint markers on the floor to prevent him from tumbling into the orchestra pit. Knowing that he had been discovered by Noël Coward, I mentioned that, although I had not been fortunate enough to meet him, I had always had an affinity to "the Master" because my first acting job was in one of the first plays he had written, and when he died in Jamaica we were staying just a few miles away. The theater abounds with Noël Coward stories, but, encouraged by the convivial atmosphere, I told Sir John a little-known anecdote that had been related to me by the producer Morton Gottlieb and took place during the out-of-town tryout of a musical. There was an ingenue in the show ... let's call her Mary Simpson ... who, at the time, was married to her manager. The manager went to the producer and said that his wife would like an "and" in front of her name on the posters and newspaper ads. In other words, it would read "And Mary Simpson." The producer said he would have to ask Noël Coward about that. The request for an "and" was presented to Coward, who, in his clipped British speech, promptly said: "Definitely not. Possibly a 'But.'" Sir John, a generous audience, loved the story, which made *my* day.

Bogged down with all my producing duties at my summer-stock company, I never had time to actually study lines, but, thanks to my ability to quickly absorb material, I only ran into memory problems on one occasion. Our schedule was to close a play on Saturday night, spend Sunday putting up the new set, have a technical rehearsal in the evening and a dress rehearsal on Monday afternoon, and open on Monday night. One Sunday night the actress who was to play the leading role in the next production had an appendicitis attack and it was apparent that she wouldn't be able to perform during the coming week. The only solution, arrived at on Monday morning, was to hold over the play from the previous week. We hastily erected the old set, and I prepared to play the part I had already performed for eight performances. Five minutes before the curtain went up I explained to the audience what had happened and went backstage to wait for my entrance. It was then that it hit me that I had forgotten every line. Evidently, once my brain believed a run was over, it cleaned house by simply blotting out the old play as it focused on the new one. Fortunately, I was not playing a leading role and managed to stagger through the performance, giving the rest of the cast only mild heart attacks.

This memory quirk has stayed with me, and once a project is finished I have trouble recalling the lines I have said or even written. Recently, the actor Tom Troupe, who played in *Same Time, Next Year* for over two years, was visiting and happened to mention a line from the play. I said, "I didn't write that." When he insisted, I said, "No, I wouldn't write a line like that. The rhythm is all wrong." Without another word, he went to my bookshelf, pulled the play down, and pointed out the line. This happens to me with TV shows I have written and sometimes, when channel surfing, I will come across an episode I have written, and I am not only unfamiliar with the lines but don't remember how the plot ends.

Our time as young producers was all very character building, but this rapid maturation took its toll, and over the twenty-five weeks I lost twenty pounds and my hair began to turn gray. Miraculously, in the fall we found that, although we had lost our original capital, we had no outstanding debts and departed for Toronto vowing never to invest money in the theater again.

There still wasn't much call for English character juveniles on television, but Jill's career continued to flourish until it was abruptly halted by her pregnancy with our first child. After a few scary weeks, I was cast in my first TV role and, although my career didn't exactly take off, I managed to eke out a living with the aid of three months as Clarabell the Clown on the Canadian version of *Howdy Doody* and a number of demeaning jobs common to most struggling young actors. A tour of *The Moon Is Blue*, with Austin Willis and Kate Reid, helped us financially survive the birth of our daughter, Laurel.

Although my name wasn't even close to being up in lights yet, all my jobs from this point on were at least vaguely related to show business. One in particular is hard to forget. I had been hired by an advertising agency to hand out leaflets on the streets of Toronto dressed as a knight in a full suit of armor. I deposited my clothes in the ad agency offices, donned the armor, and, secure in the knowledge that the helmet and visor would prevent any friends from recognizing me, sallied forth onto the streets. When I returned at the end of the day to change back into my own clothes, I found that everyone had gone home and the office was locked. With no money in my pockets—I *had* no pockets—I was reduced to trying to explain my plight to passersby and beg for enough change for my fare home. Three times I only got as far as, "You might be wondering why I'm dressed like this," but the fourth person I accosted gravely listened to my spiel and then wordlessly handed me a subway token. I clanked onto a train and, clutching my lance, took my place among the commuting straphangers. Of course, they noticed that I wasn't exactly the man in the gray flannel suit, but it was typical of Canadians that nobody said a word, which made my embarrassment even more acute. It was rather like a hippopotamus being in the room but nobody wanting to talk about it. All the way home I vowed to get into another line of work. Eventually, I did and used this incident in an episode on the TV series *Love on a Rooftop*. It was called "My Husband, the Knight."

Ever since the advent of the medium I had made a few stabs at writing television plays, but the style and form had always eluded me. Then, by chance, in 1957 I happened upon a collection of TV plays by Paddy Chayefsky, brilliantly illuminated by a number of essays about his work, which clarified the one-hour play form for me. At the time I was acting in *Anniversary Waltz* at the Crest Theatre in Toronto in a role that only appeared in the first and third acts. I used my second-act respite in my dressing room to complete a sweet, intimate comedy-drama called *The Prizewinner*, which contained a leading role for myself. After all, I was still an actor. The play was about a boring man whose saving grace was that he *knew* he was boring (my mother-in-law ingenuously said it was marvelous the way I was able to capture myself). He buys a raffle ticket, and at an office party someone thinks it would be a funny idea to phone and tell him that he has won the raffle. After that, drink makes them forget what they've done. The man, believing he is now rich, goes out and buys gifts for everyone. They still don't have the guts to tell him the truth. Once the practical joke is revealed, he believes that a girl with whom he has fallen in love was in on the joke.

I submitted the script to the Canadian Broadcasting Corporation (CBC) and anxiously awaited the call that would inform me they had bought the play and hired me to play the lead. Six weeks passed without even an acknowledgment of the receipt of my script, so I sent the play, without much hope of success, to a New York talent agency I had vaguely heard of called MCA. Three days later an agent named Jay Sanford phoned me to say that not only had he read the script but that he had sold it to a TV series called *Matinee Theater* for two thousand dollars. I didn't believe him. Positive that the call was a practical joke by a friend who liked to disguise his voice, I just kept yelling, "Get off the phone, Frank!" After fifteen minutes of Mr. Sanford earnestly insisting that he was legitimate I said, "Okay, if you are who you say you are, tell me the plot of the play." He did. Our future relationship never quite recovered from this conversation and I noticed he always had a wary look in his eyes whenever we met. However, at the time my elation outweighed my embarrassment and the next day I went to the CBC to retrieve my script. Of course, I was not entirely successful in keeping a note of gloating out of my voice when I told them why I wanted it back, and their indignation at my "unprofessional" behavior of submitting my play to more than one producer didn't exactly move me to tears. Claiming they couldn't locate my script immediately they asked me to come back in an hour, and when I did they, not too surprisingly, had decided they also wanted to produce the play. It was typical of the Canadian character to require validation from another source, preferably another country, before making any commitment.

It was agreed that the CBC production would be aired first, but since I was not hired to play the part I had written for myself, I felt that perhaps "somebody was trying to tell me something." I loved working as an actor but always resented the fact that any opportunity to practice my craft was always in someone else's hands, and this latest rejection made me decide to concentrate on a writing career. Writers can be self-starters, which suited my personality.

The live CBC broadcast of *The Prizewinner* was a nightmare. The network lost twenty minutes of the sound portion of the show and since they had also mislaid the "trouble is temporary" sign, I spent the hour either watching actors silently mouthing my lines or kicking our innocent TV set. Despite this less-than-perfect debut, the play was a solid first rung in my writing career and it was later produced on two U.S. networks, once with Arthur Hill and Teresa Wright in a U.S. Steel Hour production. It was also given a second production on the CBC, starring Peter Lind Hayes, and was shown on the BBC in England, and even produced on French TV.

Even though over the next five years I wrote fourteen TV plays for the CBC, with most of them subsequently being produced by the American networks during the tail end of live shows from New York, the fees were not enough to live on, so I augmented our income by writing over a hundred variety shows. These endeavors, combined with Jill's earnings from appearances on some TV variety and drama shows, enabled us to buy a house, have Christopher, our second child, and then buy an even bigger house. Knowing my peripatetic background one didn't have to be from Vienna to understand the psychological roots of this "edifice complex," which was to stay with me for many years.

Our decision to buy another house was prompted by a desire to move closer to downtown Toronto, but, seduced by a very grand split-level new home on a treed three-acre lot, we ended up buying even further out in the country. The house was extraordinary, as was the price. Foolishly secure in the knowledge that the weekly variety TV shows I had been writing would continue, we blithely took possession of the house we believed would be our home for the rest of our lives. Three days after moving in we compounded the mistake by leaving for a two-month trip to Europe. We left Laurie with Jill's family and Christopher with mine—another mistake because, although they got along fine without us, they missed each other. Nervous about our children being orphaned if we were in a plane crash, we opted to make the major legs of our journey by ship or train. Still suffering from delusions of grandeur, quite inconceivably, we decided to travel first class.

We sailed from New York on the *Queen Elizabeth* and, after some wonderful times with old friends and family in England, traveled through France, Switzerland, and Italy by train. Towards the end of the trip, our cash almost exhausted, we arrived one evening at the Villa D'Este at Lake Como, where we took one look at the elegant guests, all clad in either dinner jackets or formal gowns, and resolved not to order any food in the hotel during our entire weekend stay. We bought some bread and cheese in a neighboring village, smuggled the food into our room, and resolutely declined all suggestions by the staff that we dine or breakfast in the lavish hotel restaurant. I did notice the puzzled expression on the chamber-maid's face when she encountered bread crumbs and bits of cheese in our bed, but my embarrassment ran a poor second to the fear that we would have to wash dishes to pay for exorbitant room-service bills. On Monday morning when we checked out we learned that all meals were included in the price of the room.

We set sail from England in a ship that would dock in Montreal, where we would take a train to Toronto. Although traveling first class, the voyage was made extremely tense for us because we only had about fifteen dollars left, which was not nearly enough to tip the stewards at the end of the trip. The night before we were to dock, Jill decided to go for broke and gambled all our money at blackjack. Miraculously, she won! Wisely, she quit while she was ahead, and the tension in my neck and four-day indigestion final-ly subsided. We tipped the staff and arrived at Toronto's Union Station with only the proverbial one thin dime, which I used to phone a friend who picked us up in his car.

Some months later, while at work, I got a call from Jill, who happily said, "Before we left for Europe I was afraid we might run out of money. Well, I was just going through my wallet and remembered it had a secret compartment. Guess what? I'd com-pletely forgotten I'd hidden three hundred dollars in there in case of an emergency. Isn't that terrific?" I didn't think so. She said, "Oh, I know we had a few bad moments on the ship, but now we have three hundred dollars we didn't have before. Isn't that great?" I didn't think that, either.

The day after we arrived home I phoned the Canadian Broad-casting Corporation to see what series I'd be working on that year and was told that they didn't have a show for me. I had trouble replacing the phone, but when I did, I looked around at the most-ly unfurnished twelve rooms of our new house and tried to absorb the fact that we were in way over our heads financially. As an actor,

I'd learned never to have a monthly "nut" that couldn't be paid even when going through a dry spell, so the clammy feeling in my stomach was laced with anger at my own stupidity.

The situation was precarious and every morning I would trudge through the snow to our mailbox at the end of the country road in the hope that it would contain a residual check. More often than not, the lock on the box would be frozen and I'd have to thaw it out with a flame from a lighter, adding a few more minutes of suspense, not to mention frozen ears and fingertips. Eventually, we dug ourselves out of the financial hole, but the experience provided a painful lesson that has stayed with me. Since then, we have lived very well but always within our means.

I spent the next two years scrambling around trying to feed our huge mortgage by writing everything from soap operas to panel shows. One of these was called *Flashback* and had a simple premise: three once very famous people were guests on the show and a panel of four had to guess who they were. I indulged myself by booking many old Hollywood movie stars. We used to tape two shows in the same evening, and my job was to take the six guests out to a restaurant and prepare them for the show. We had some astounding combinations at those dinners, and one night I remember the group consisted of Francis X. Bushman, Ramon Navarro, Gloria Swanson, Paulette Goddard, Mae Murray, and Agnes Moorhead. They kept talking about "Rudi" and it took me a while to realize they were talking about Valentino.

After moving to LA my curiosity about old Hollywood was greatly satisfied during my tennis games with the actor, director, and producer Norman Lloyd, who just turned eighty-five. I realize that the age of eighty-five and the game of tennis are not a normal pairing, but Norman is not a "normal" man. During his illustrious career he has worked with Orson Welles and the Mercury Theater, Alfred Hitchcock (he was one of the stars of *Saboteur*), and Charlie

Chaplin. We used to play on what I called "famous dead people's courts," alternating between the Ira Gershwin and William Wyler houses. One day Norman indicated a house next door and mentioned that he used to play with Charlie Chaplin there. I asked what was Chaplin really like. He thought for a moment and then said, "Good forehand, no overhead."

Our son, Christopher, was something of a childhood tennis prodigy and began beating me when he was about nine. He is now a writer, and the first short story he ever sold was called "Tennis or What?" and concerned itself with the first time a boy beats his father at tennis. Sometimes people would ask me if I minded being beaten so soundly and regularly by Chris. Silly question—any chagrin I might have had was far outweighed by the pride in the prowess of my son. Anyway, I really don't care if I win or lose. Having been an actor, I just cared if I looked good!

This time, in the early sixties, was highlighted by the production of my second play, *A Very Close Family*. A drama about internecine warfare and heavily influenced by Arthur Miller's *Death of a Salesman*, it opened at the Manitoba Theatre Centre in Winnipeg, where, although it was well received, I felt it lacked the impact I had envisioned. Always willing to revise a script to make it more effective, I was prevented from further work because of my indecision about whether the production's faults were caused by some of the casting or by flaws in the text. Casting is always crucial and an actor, even though talented, can sink any play if unsuited to a role. Fortunately, some nine months later, the play was given a marvelous ninety-minute production on the CBC. It was directed by Harvey Hart and had a brilliant cast headed by that great movie and stage star Melvyn Douglas. He was the most pleasant of men (he loved writers!), with a piercing intelligence; it was a joy to watch him work. The rest of the cast included Tom Bosley (who later became even more well known by appearing on *Happy Days*),

Gordon Pinsent, Charmion King, and Jill. I was pleased to see that the problems in Winnipeg were more the result of miscasting than of any intrinsic weakness of the play.

Since the play was a thinly disguised piece about Jill's family, I arranged for the television version to be broadcast only during the two months that her mother and father were away in Florida. We were apprehensive about other family members seeing it, and for quite a while I answered the phone in a disguised voice, but as time went by we thought we'd "gotten away with it." Then one night a niece came over to baby-sit and told us the family had been meeting twice a week to discuss the play. To this day, none of the family has ever admitted to me that they saw it.

By now it was apparent that there was no professional future for me in Canada, and we decided to pull up stakes and follow a number of our colleagues to Hollywood, which had become the center of almost all TV and film activity. It is a peculiar phenomenon that so many Canadian artists from this period only achieved international reputations by moving to another country. The simple explanation for this mass exodus was the Canadian attitude of, "If you're so good, why are you still here?" but the actual reasons are more complicated. The lack of identity caused by living in the shadow of a powerful neighbor, while also maintaining strong cultural ties to the mother country of Britain, seems to have produced an inferiority complex, which in turn makes it difficult for Canadians to make a commitment to their own artists. This insecurity is aggravated by the belief that the arts are a luxury, not a necessity. This completely misses the point that without artists to hold up a mirror to their society, Canadians will never have a national identity. It is no accident that the most important theater in Canada produces plays by Shakespeare, and the second most prominent one is devoted to the works of Shaw. No wonder Canadian writers left in droves. The Canadian public has ambivalent attitudes about outside recognition of their native-born talent: they are proud of their success but also resentful that they "left home." This schizophrenia has resulted in the work of Canadian expatriates generally receiving their worst press in the country of their birth. As one writer put it, "We are the only country who eats its young." One thing is clear: if you can succeed in Canada, anywhere else is easy.

★ Hollywood: where you're terrific if you're even good ★

★ Upon arriving in Los Angeles in 1964 I learned that a producer named Danny Arnold, who was about to launch a new television series called *Bewitched*, wanted to meet with me. His interest had come about because my agents had given him a play of mine that had been produced at Toronto's Crest Theatre. It was called *Simon Says Get Married*, a comedy about computer dating which, when first produced in 1960, was treated by the critics as science fiction. Being ahead of its time was not the play's only problem. This was my first stage play and, afraid that the audience wouldn't laugh, I had put in a joke about every four seconds. Well, they laughed at everything—and didn't like the play much because I'd sacrificed character and believability for the sake of laughs. It was a painful lesson but with a wonderful payoff, as it brought me to the attention of Danny Arnold, which in turn led me to ten years of lucrative employment at Columbia, at Screen Gems Studios. Another lesson: good things can happen from failure because show business works in unpredictable ways.

After looking at the pilot film of *Bewitched* I came up with about twelve premises (if you don't like this, wait a minute) and pitched them to Danny the next day, and he commissioned me to write one about Halloween, which introduced the character of Aunt Clara, the bumbling witch, charmingly played by Marion Lorne.

My meeting was on Tuesday and I casually asked, "You're not in any great hurry for this, are you?" Just as casually, he said, "No, Friday'll be fine." Friday? Three days away? In Canada it used to take me six weeks to write a script, but, believing this was the way things were done in Hollywood, I wrote feverishly for seventy-two hours straight and, bleary-eyed, returned with a finished script on Friday morning. When Danny asked me what I was doing there, I answered, "You said Friday." He said, "I meant *next* Friday—and I didn't expect it then."

As I entered my room at the Chateau Marmont Hotel a half hour later the phone was ringing. It was Danny, who had already read my script, calling to commission me to write six more. The next day I was also offered a job as a story editor on a new series starring Robert Cummings and Julie Newmar about a robot, called *My Living Doll.* Within a few days of arriving in LA I had more financial security than in all my years in Canada.

After a quick trip back to Toronto to put our house up for rent and secure immigration green cards, the four of us and our golden retriever, Simon, flew back to LA, where we moved into the Chateau Marmont for a month while we looked for a furnished house to rent. We found a pleasant, modest house with a pool in Brentwood, an LA suburb that was to become nationally known some thirty years later through the O. J. Simpson murder trial. We were fortunate in that we had been preceded in Hollywood by many Canadian writers and performers so, surrounded by this group of supportive friends, the transition from one country to another wasn't as traumatic as it might have been. The children learned how to swim and started school, and I drove off to the studio every day in a new lemon-colored Jaguar to seek fame and fortune.

I discovered I was a good literary mimic, an important element in writing TV series episodes in which one is re-creating already established characters, and so the work came easily to me. It didn't deter me at all that I was writing scripts for the characters of a witch and a robot, and found myself in story conferences where grown men would earnestly ask, "Would a witch do that?" or "Is this a believable line for a robot?" I had quickly grasped that to succeed as a TV writer one had to suspend disbelief and never "write down" but, working within the confines of the television formula, devote one's full energies and talents to the projects at hand. I enjoyed plying my craft and, frankly, also felt I'd been given a license to print money.

Situation comedy or "comedy of situation" has been around for centuries, but the modern "sitcoms" were inherited from radio, which, I assume, took the format from vaudeville sketches. The format of half-hour or hour shows also came from that medium because that is how blocks of advertising were sold. A half-hour show actually only has twenty-four minutes of playing time, with the rest of the time being taken up by commercials. The format of a TV situation comedy is quite simple: a short teaser, followed by two acts, and ending with a brief epilogue. In writing them the trick is to explore character (usually in a simplistic way ... we only have twenty-four minutes) while making the characters relentlessly endearing, develop the springboard setup in the teaser, and be very, very funny.

When I started writing in Hollywood almost all shows were on film. Using one camera, they mimicked the technique of feature films except that they were shot in a limited number of sets, which could be used every week. Although the scripts, under the guidance of a story editor, usually went through a rewrite and a polish, once the three-and-a-half-day shooting started they were almost never rewritten. The bulk of the shows were written by freelancers and the "top of the show" was three thousand dollars an episode.

This was all changed by the three-camera shows (actually four but, for some reason, still referred to as three) such as *All in the*

Family and *Maude.* Multiple video cameras using tape rather than film allowed a show to be shot in one evening. Staffs of writers were hired who cowrote the shows and, after an initial reading by the cast, constantly rewrote the lines right up until the actual taping in front of a live studio audience. This mimicked the theater (or a play in desperate trouble on the road!) rather than the feature film.

All the shows I created or wrote were one-camera (it would be hard to do the special effects of *Bewitched* or *The Flying Nun* in front of an audience) and, years later, when I was talked into returning to television for a brief spell, I decided to follow the progress of a three-camera show for a week. Each night the writers, sometimes as many as six or eight, were closeted in a room laden with take-out food and, in an intensely competitive atmosphere, screamed out lines in an attempt to get them into the script. This method of working quickly burns out writers (the pastrami alone will kill you) and, because of the dreadful hours, is lethal to many marriages. One night a week a "comedy consultant" comes in to "punch up" the script and for about five hours' work is paid the amazing amount of thirteen thousand dollars (no, this is not a misprint). At the end of the week, after pages of rewrites, I didn't think the script was any better. Different perhaps, but not better. This killing schedule makes writing situation comedy today very much a young person's game.

When I worked in television we worked at a much more leisurely pace, with everyone home with their families by seven o'clock. My God, we even went out for lunch! We also did thirty-nine shows as opposed to twenty-two, and although they weren't all wonderful (far from it), I believe they were as good as the present crop, which sometimes seem as if they are written by naughty children being "daring" by including dirty words.

However, when reading this, you must bear in mind that I'm very much a "why did they have to take the running boards off of cars?" sort of guy with a rose-colored rearview mirror who doesn't believe that any changes made during the past fifty years have added to the quality of life in any way.

That first year (nothing if not ambitious) I wrote over twenty half-hour episodes and the following fall was offered the job of story editor on *Bewitched*, along with the opportunity to write pilot films for new series. Danny Arnold had left *Bewitched* and the job of producer had been given to Jerry Davis.

When I first met Jerry he was a slim, pixie-ish man in his late forties of great charm and sartorial elegance. Only half-jokingly, he sometimes referred to himself as "the Jewish Cary Grant." In the play *Tribute* I described him as a mixture of Noël Coward, Peter Pan, and the Marx Brothers.

Within minutes of my arrival, he appeared in the doorway of my office and told me he was suffering from a terrible case of hemorrhoids. Since he felt it was not an attractive condition he made me promise to be discreet about this knowledge and not "spread it around." I said it wasn't the sort of information I ever used as a conversation starter. Reassured, he invited me to lunch at the Columbia executive dining room. As we were walking past one of the sound stages we passed three grips sitting on the roof eating box lunches. One yelled down, "Hey Jerry, how's the ass?" So much for discretion. He later had an operation to relieve his delicate condition, and when he was wheeled back to his room he demanded to see the baby because "for that much pain you should have something to show for it!"

Jerry was a world-class hypochondriac. One night he awoke to "discover" a dent in the middle of his chest and rushed to the phone to call his beleaguered doctor, who agreed to meet him at his office. The doctor took a look at Jerry's chest, rolled up his own shirt, and said, "Oh look, I've got one too. *Everybody's* got one!"

The year we worked together was one of the most enjoyable of my life, mostly due to Jerry, who, although somewhat allergic to work, expended great efforts in planning our social activities each day, which always included long lunches at the Brown Derby or Musso and Frank's, where he would regale me with stories about his days at MGM in the late forties, when he was writing Esther Williams movies and such sagas as *The Cult of the Cobra*. His first wife was from the family that owned the May Company and he freely admitted that her social contacts helped him to get started at Metro when he got out of the army. In those days there was time to indulge in having people around just because their presence gave pleasure, and Jerry certainly fit that job description. Although not without talent (he had sold short stories to the *New Yorker* and other magazines), he found it much more pleasant to be a sophisticated court jester than to sweat over a fourteenth rewrite. This order of priorities had stayed with him and he never seemed able to take himself or his work seriously. One time we were interrupted at lunch by a frantic assistant producer, who said that the screening room was filled with people, waiting for Jerry to view dailies. He turned to me with an expression of distaste and said, "You know, this is the part I *hate*."

After his divorce from his first wife, Nancy, with whom he had a son, Jeffrey, he married the actress Marilyn Maxwell, had another son, Matthew, and later would marry a wonderful woman, Beryl, and father two more sons, Josh and Tony. But when I met him he was between marriages and a great deal of his day was spent arranging various dates for the evening with assorted actresses, starlets, and models. Almost incapable of spending an evening alone, he sometimes "overbooked," and I often had the mental image of three women under hair driers in various parts of the city, all believing they would be having dinner with Jerry that night. Although he enjoyed a reputation as a ladies' man, I believe his enjoyment lay more in wining and dining rather than in the actual sex. However, his romantic real life was like my fantasy life. One time I was talking to an attractive actress on the Columbia lot when Jerry joined us and, courteous as always, introduced himself by saying, "I'm Jerome Davis." The girl looked at him unbelievingly for a moment and then said, "Jerry, we lived together for a year!" He later claimed that he hadn't recognized her because she "had taken off a lot of weight."

When he remarried, our wives became close friends, and over the years we traveled the world together with this man who never failed to amaze us.

Now, I don't want to leave the impression that Jerry was only obsessed with superficial pleasures, because he was a complex man with his share of guilt about not working to develop his talent, and there is no question that he suffered remorse at the pain his sometimes irresponsible behavior had caused his family. It was this complexity that made me sense there was a rich theatrical personality in Jerry, but this feeling didn't crystalize into the fictional character of Scottie Templeton in *Tribute* until years after I met him.

During these years of television work I remained at Columbia Studios creating or developing a number of series. We bought a large Spanish house on Tigertail Road in Brentwood and five years later, still indulging my "Tara" penchant for mansions, a miniestate with a tennis court a few blocks away on North Saltair.

The first pilot script I wrote was about a young married couple living in San Francisco and became the series *Love on a Rooftop*, which starred Peter Duell and Judy Carne. The supporting cast included Rich Little, whom I had known in Canada when he was just starting out as an impressionist. Many impressionists use their talent for mimicry as a stepping-stone to careers as actors or comedians. Not Rich. Although a very good light-comedy actor, he was obsessed with perfecting his uncanny imitations and rarely seemed to speak in his own voice. This habit could be annoying to others within earshot, as being addressed in the not-quite-perfect-yet voice of John Wayne for hours on end could be a trifle wearing, but Rich was relentless. He also never stopped adding new voices to his repertoire. One weekend Jill and I stayed with him at a house he was renting in Las Vegas while he was appearing at one of the casinos. We returned to the house early one morning to find Rich staring intently at the TV screen. He turned to us with a look of triumph; "I got him! I can do Wendell Corey!"

E. W. Swackhamer, known to all and sundry as "Swack," and who would work brilliantly on most of my future shows, produced and directed the series with many of the episodes being shot in San Francisco, which gave the series a nice, jaunty air. I stayed on as story editor, wrote some sixteen episodes, and enjoyed the year of working on the series—of all the series I created I like *Love on a Rooftop* the best. This was because it managed to combine fresh, unpredictable comedy with great charm. We were all sorry we weren't picked up for a second year ... we lost out to *That Girl*, even though I believe our ratings were higher ... but I didn't have time to mourn too long as I was already wrestling with the script of *The Flying Nun*.

The genesis of *The Flying Nun* was a slim book written by a Puerto Rican housewife, called *The Fifteenth Pelican*, which was unearthed in a bookstore by Norman Kurland. Norman later became my film agent but was then an assistant to Harry Ackerman, an executive producer at Screen Gems. While shooting *Love on a Rooftop* on location in San Francisco, Harry, Jill, and I were riding in the backseat of a taxi one day and Harry asked me what I thought about the idea for a show of a nun who could fly. After I pantomimed throwing up he turned to get Jill's opinion, who said, "I don't know, I think it's sort of cute." A few weeks later we were ensconced in an obscenely expensive hotel suite in San Juan, which cleverly obligated me to write the script. This was an old studio trick but new to me: get the writer so beholden to the studio he won't have the nerve to back out.

I did have some demands, however, one being that I would only write the script if Sally Field would star in it. I had seen her in the television series *Gidget* and believed that her natural charm and ability to play a bit of a hell-raiser would diminish the treacle that was in the premise of a show about nuns. The studio agreed, but, at the last moment, the deal with Sally stalled and we started shooting with another young actress. After three days it became apparent that the show wasn't going to work with this actress and the studio prepared to shut down shooting. I don't know what changed Sally's mind (although I suspect that the new red Ferrari she was soon seen driving around town had something to do with it), but she suddenly agreed to play Sister Bertrille and the show came alive.

I had sometimes heard of actors whom "the camera loves," but I had never seen this demonstrated until I had looked at film of Sally. She simply leaps right off the screen at you, which, along with her natural talent, explains why someone who, although pretty, is not beautiful in the classic Hollywood sense and has an ordinary voice became such a big star. The opposite is also true: some talented actors who are great to look at and have pleasant, well-trained voices simply "disappear" when in front of a camera. All very unfair, but one of the realities of the business.

The idea for *The Partridge Family* was triggered by a number of events. While in Canada I had written a television play called *The Big Coin Sound*, which was about a vocal group. Then one night I happened to catch a family group called The Cowsills on *The Tonight Show*. Since *The Sound of Music* was enormously popular at the time, I thought the combination of original music and comedy could be very effective in a television series.

We were fortunate in our casting, with Danny Bonaduce, an extremely talented child actor, providing the comedy sparks, the talented David Cassidy (with the help of clever merchandising) becoming a teenage rock star, Susan Dey being every young boy's romantic fantasy, and Shirley Jones providing the attractive glue to the piece. David Madden was given the task of adding a dash of bitters if things got too sugary, and he did it perfectly. Later in the series we managed to get Ray Bolger to play the character of Shirley's father, which was based almost entirely upon my own father. Apart from all the commercial elements, I believe the scripts were sweetly moralistic without being preachy, and perhaps this is why the series ran for four years and is still seen regularly on syndicated television.

Bridget Loves Bernie was the story of a mixed marriage between a Gentile woman, played by Meredith Baxter, and a Jewish man, played by David Birney. It is hard to imagine today that this good-natured piece was in any way controversial or offensive, and the fact of the matter is that it was neither of those things. Audiences seemed to like the show, but a small faction of Orthodox Jews objected to us showing a mixed marriage in which the two people were happy. I remember being at a Variety Club lunch in Toronto where a rabbi, tongue in cheek, said, "I understand we have a man on the dais who, in his honor, had three thousand trees uprooted in Israel." Very funny, but the objections of this extremely small portion of the population made the brass at CBS uncomfortable, and they canceled the show while it was in the top ten. Probably a first and a last.

The Girl with Something Extra was about a woman with highly developed ESP, and reunited me with Sally Field. Her husband was played by John Davidson and the cast included Jack Sheldon, who is not only a wonderful comic actor but also one of the greatest trumpet players in the world. I wrote only about three of the scripts as, by the time the series aired, I was already working on the next pilot project. I realized that my not staying with a series meant the possibility of it not being produced exactly as I would have liked, but this risk was offset by not having to write the same characters week after week. I even get bored *watching* the same characters on a weekly basis, let alone writing them, and have always found it hard to understand how a writer, even though he is being paid a fortune, can slog away at the same series over a number of years. Anyway, *The Girl with Something Extra* didn't seem to suffer from my absence as it was well acted and produced. But it only lasted one season.

I believe that some of the pilot scripts I wrote that were filmed but never made it onto the network schedule were better than the ones that did become series. One of these was called *The Princess and Me,* and was about a European princess who wants to spend some time in the United States as an ordinary person but is frustrated in this goal by the State Department, who assigns a secret service man to shadow her. Barbara Hershey, a blindingly talented young actress, eventually played the princess. Barbara was just about the most serious actress I'd ever worked with, and the results of this single-minded devotion to her craft were later on display in a series of really remarkable performances in both television and film. I liked her and her passionate approach to acting enormously, even though I quickly became aware that comedy was not her strong point and that it was a good idea to explain the jokes. I'm sorry that our paths have not crossed since, but, alas, that is common in show business. Before Barbara was cast as the Princess we auditioned dozens of actresses but couldn't find anyone who everyone could agree was right for the role. About this time the studio temporarily let me out of my contract to write a TV adaption of the play *The Moon Is Blue,* which was to be shot in London. I was very well suited to this assignment as, years before, I had toured as an actor in the play and was also familiar with London.

Screen Gems suggested that while I was there I audition some British actresses for the part of the Princess, which I proceeded to do in the Connaught Hotel, where I was staying.

After one of these sessions, the associate producer on *The Moon Is Blue* project asked me what I was doing. When I told him, he mentioned that he was dating a Princess and asked me if I'd like to have lunch with her. Now, this young man was very "show business" and I assumed he was dating someone along the lines of an exotic dancer. Anyway, I agreed to join them for lunch and was introduced to an attractive woman who he said was "Princess Elizabeth." Now, I knew it couldn't be Princess Elizabeth because she was queen, so I proceeded to ask a lot of inane questions like, "When do you lose your country?" and "Do people have to back out of the room when leaving you?" She took all of this in good spirits and mentioned that she was living in a house where the great actress Ellen Terry had once lived and asked if I'd like to see it. While she was driving me through London in her Jaguar I asked if she used a last name and what she was listed under on her driver's license. She casually handed it to me and I read "Her Royal Highness Princess Elizabeth of Yugoslavia." Flabbergasted, I said, "You mean you're a real princess?" She said, "Yes. My father was King Paul." The door of Ellen Terry's house was answered by a pleasant woman in the traditional garb of a skirt, cashmere sweater, and pearls. She was introduced as "Mrs. Ogilvie." The phone rang and as my new best friend, Princess Elizabeth, went to answer it, I said to Mrs. Ogilvie, "Did you know she's a real princess?" She smiled and said, "Yes, I know." It turned out that Mrs. Ogilvie was Princess Alexandria. When I related this series of gaffes to my mother, who lived and died an ardent royalist, she was appalled and said, "I hope you didn't let them know you were a Canadian!" I confessed that I had excused my ignorance by masquerading as an American.

By the way, *The Moon Is Blue* was never filmed, which puzzled me, as it seemed like perfect TV fare. Years later I was told that some numbskull at the network had remembered that the movie, made by Otto Preminger a few years before, had been refused a seal of approval by some Catholic organization because it used the word "pregnant," and so it was deemed not fit for television. Well, some things do change for the better.

Many horror stories about Hollywood's brutalization of writers have been written, and I'm sure most of them are true, but I was treated better than most. This was not due to any recognition of my artistic worth or because I was a wonderful fellow but was simply a result of an ability to write shows that got onto the network schedules. Studios like anyone who can help them make millions of dollars. Still fresh from the financial uncertainties of Canada, I found this blatant commercialism rather refreshing and enthusiastically enjoyed the material rewards that are heaped upon TV writers with good track records.

However, despite my elevated status, I was not immune to the lunacies of network executives. One "creative suggestion" was received on the eve of starting to shoot a new series. This memo read: "I have been thinking about the series all weekend and I have come to a conclusion: all twenty-six episodes must be done in good taste!" I immediately sent back a telegram that read: "Thank God your memo arrived just in time. We had planned twenty-six episodes in bad taste, but of course this changes everything."

Another time, when receiving notes about a show that featured an African-American character, a rarity in those days, the executive looked up from the script and asked, "How will we know he's black?" The rest of us just looked at one another in some disbelief. Finally, I said, "We're going to cast a black actor." The network man realized that he'd looked like an idiot (I think), but executives don't like to admit they're wrong. He said, "Well, okay, but you'd better make sure he's *very* black."

Of course, it was a given that not all my projects would be successful, and the first feature film I wrote was a disaster. The title was *Stand Up and Be Counted* and it was an attempt to look at the burgeoning women's movement. Jackie Cooper directed it and Mike Frankovich, a burly ex-football player, produced it because, I strongly suspect, he saw it as a chance to put a lot of women on the screen with no bras. My recollection of working on the film is cloudy, but I do recall that during the preproduction meetings in Mike's office a man with a black bag would enter, Mike would unceremoniously drop his pants, and the man would plunge a needle into his bare buttocks. Mike would look over at me and ask, "Want one?" New to the ways of Hollywood, I didn't know what I was being offered so would reply, "No, a little too early in the day for me." Of course, they were vitamin booster shots, but who knew? Everyone in show business has had a hand in something embarrassing that will show up on TV in reruns and cause the perpetrator to rush for the remote control. Mine is *Stand Up and Be Counted.*

Jackie Cooper had been a world-famous child star and his blond hair and trembling lower lip had won the hearts of millions when he played the part of Skippy, opposite Wallace Beery, in *The Champ.* He was one of the few child actors who weathered the difficult transition from being "cute" to being a first-class adult actor. He branched off into television directing and then segued into jobs as the producer on his own series and as the president of Screen Gems Films for four years.

There is a postscript to my experience in working with him on *Stand Up and Be Counted.* For a couple of years I was a member of a group of once famous Hollywood-types who would meet informally for lunch every Thursday at a restaurant called The Caffe Roma in Beverly Hills. The "cast" included Jimmy Komack, the producer of such hit series as *Welcome Back Kotter*; Robert Clary, the diminutive Frenchman on *Hogan's Heroes*; Howie Morris, who worked with Sid Ceasar on *Your Show of Shows*; Bernie Kopell, an actor from *The Love Boat*; Ronnie Graham, from *New Faces of 1952*; and Jackie Cooper. I was about ten years younger than most of them and the litany of their medical ailments every week did get a little wearing. I stopped going when I came home one day and my wife said, "You look depressed. Were they talking about their prostates again?"

Whenever Jackie Cooper would leave to go to the bathroom Jimmy Komack would lean across the table to me and say, "He has no idea who you are, you know." I would say, "Jimmy, we were at the same studio for four years and I created a number of hit series when he was president. We spent time with him and his wife in London and I also wrote a movie he directed, so we were on location together in Denver." He would say, "That may be so, but he has no idea who you are." Now, this was a group of comedians who would say anything for a laugh, so I didn't take what he was saying seriously. Then one day the movie star Jaqueline Bisset came into the restaurant and came over to our table to say hello. After she left Jack said, "I directed her in a movie once." He then went on to recount the plot of *Stand Up and Be Counted*. I said, "Jack, I wrote it." He said, "Yeah?" I said, "Don't you remember, we were on location in Denver together?" He just looked puzzled. Jimmy grinned.

I'm not suggesting that Jackie had become senile (he's still only in his mid-seventies), but I have found that actors do tend to be a bit self-involved and they don't remember *anybody*! This is why you can be at five or six intimate dinner parties with certain actors and have to be reintroduced every time you meet them. It's a sure tip-off when people call you "Kid" or, when inquiring about your wife, ask, "How's your lovely lady?"

During my time at Screen Gems I wrote over a hundred scripts, and the years passed in a pleasant blur of work, child raising, tennis, scores of parties, and traveling. But was I happy? Of course. At least I thought so. The only dissonant note was my being afflicted with a series of debilitating cluster migraine headaches. My guess, aided by hindsight, is that these were probably caused by a deeply suppressed dissatisfaction with the scripts I was writing. It wasn't that I believed I was a great writer but that, given the low aim of TV programming, I wasn't being asked to do my best work. I tried to resolve the internal conflict by setting aside three months of every year to work on scripts that were not tailored to someone else's specifications, but although two of these screenplays were sold and a play, *Fling!*, was published, the headaches persisted. Not for the first time the theater came to my rescue when I wrote *Same Time, Next Year.*

★ Same Time, Next Year: once a great notion ★

I finished the first draft of *Same Time, Next Year*, then called *Same Time, Same Place*, at the end of July 1974, and it opened on Broadway on March 13, 1975 ... an incredibly short period in a medium where events usually move with the speed of a line at the post office. Was it the smooth, sweet ride everyone assumed it to be? Well, yes and no.

Writers are often asked where an idea originated. I always answer honestly, "I don't know." This is because plays rarely, if ever, drop into the brain fully formed and ready to write but are usually a combination of notions assembled, often through trial and error and with journeys down dead ends, over a period of months or even years into a cohesive premise. My plays generally start with a character or situation. *Same Time* is the only one that started with a setting.

Some time in the early seventies Jill and I were on a driving trip through Northern California and checked into an inn called The Heritage House, just south of the small town of Mendocino. When I walked into the charming room furnished with antiques and a grand piano, and featuring an open fireplace that housed a stack of burning logs and a window with a view overlooking the picturesque coastline more reminiscent of Maine than California, it immediately reminded me of a stage setting. I had not thought of writing for the theater for some time, but, perhaps because a certain disenchantment with working in television had set in, over the next couple of days it occurred to me that this would be the perfect setting for a romantic comedy. This notion of a romantic comedy came about not only because that was a genre I enjoyed watching but because, as a writer, it was a field in which I felt comfortable.

The idea that it should be a two-character play is also easily understood. I had been restricted for some years to writing scripts that, due to the constraints of television, were only twenty-four minutes long, which didn't allow for any character development. I felt that using only two people in a full-length play would provide the time needed to give them some complexities and let them breathe.

The isolation and tranquility of our few days' stay away from the stress of raising children, car pooling, home owning, and the normal ups and downs of a long marriage gradually brought about a euphoric relaxation. Able to devote ourselves solely to each other, the faces of mother, father, mature university student, and television writer that we daily presented to the world gradually slipped away and we were able to connect in a profound way as simply ourselves. But as a writer I was never able to totally shut off being not only a participant in but also an observer of my life, and this experience triggered the beginning of an idea for a play.

My daydreaming, which is what constructing fiction is mostly about, led me to the idea of making it a "life cycle" play, where we would see the characters over a period of years. This, in turn, led to the central core of two lovers who meet every year in a remote location. I also flirted with the idea that the political events of the country should in some way shape their characters, but that's as far as I got and I put the notion on the back burner as we returned to "real life" and I started to write a half-hour TV pilot film.

The idea flitted in and out of my consciousness over the next few months but never expanded into anything I could really get excited about. At one point I had the thought that we watch these two lovers over the years only to discover at the end of the play that they are actually married, but one weekend a year they became other characters. Then I learned that Harold Pinter had worked the same territory in a short play called *The Lovers*, and I abandoned the idea because I thought this denouement in a full-length play would really irritate an audience.

Then one morning while I was shaving, not even aware I was thinking of the play, it fell into my head: the two characters should be happily married to other people. At the beginning of the play they fall into a one-night stand that, over the years, blossoms into an affair and eventually a friendship kept alive by a one-weekend-a-year tryst. The perfect romantic fantasy!

The hair on the back of my neck actually felt as if it was standing up. The idea was so simple and so right that a few minutes later I became afraid that somebody must have thought of it before. This, I believe, is a fear all writers have when they think of a premise that excites them. In this case, though, because Jill and I had started our careers as actors and between us had appeared in some four hundred plays, had seen twice that many, and couldn't think of a similar premise, I felt on safe ground. Of course, the events of each scene had to be devised, but the play was screaming to be written. Unfortunately, this was not possible at the moment as my time and efforts were committed to writing and producing a pilot film for Columbia Studios.

For close to ten years I had been working under a series of three-year contracts for Columbia/Screen Gems, which called for me to write three pilot films a year. This arrangement had worked out well for all concerned as I had been well paid and pretty much left alone to create, while the studio had benefited by seven of my pilot scripts becoming fully fledged series that generated huge flows of cash. But shortly before getting the idea for *Same Time* I had balked at signing a new contract for a number of reasons. The main one was that although I was supposed to receive twenty-five percent of the profits of my shows, to that date (and even this date) I had not received one cent. This, despite the fact that one show, *The Partridge Family*, had been on the air for four seasons and had also made millions from merchandising and music recordings. My business manager, who taught an accounting course at UCLA, once used the accounting statement sent to me by the studio as an example of "the most creative writing in Hollywood."

After my refusing to resign a contract, the studio had spent three months wooing me with promises of more money, a studio car, bonuses, a newly decorated office, baseball tickets … in short, every "perk" a major studio could offer. I finally signed.

The first film I was to write and executive produce was called *Everything Money Can't Buy*, about an angel who, every week, would return to earth and affect the lives of ordinary mortals. It was regarded as a "soft" script, which, in TV terms, meant it dealt in relationships rather than hard action or broad comedy. I gather that the network was willing to take a chance because they felt the charm of the script would offset the lack of pratfalls.

The production came together quickly, with Jose Ferrer cast as the angel in the series' only running part. Jose, or Joe as most of his friends called him, had become internationally famous playing Toulouse-Lautrec in the film *Moulin Rouge*. I had been fortunate in seeing him on stage when he played his signature role of Cyrano de Bergerac. He confided to me that one night he forgot to stick on the huge nose that is integral to the role. And nobody noticed!

The other roles were to be played by guest stars Brenda Vaccaro, Bert Convy, and Peter Bonerz. Carl Reiner was set to direct. The public knows Carl primarily as a wonderful sketch player who appeared with Sid Ceasar in *Your Show of Shows* and as the creator/writer of the *Dick Van Dyke* series, but he also has a lesser-known talent:

he is a marvelous emcee. His easy, informal manner enlivens any social gathering, and I was looking forward to being on location with him. We all traveled to San Francisco, where the opening show was to be shot.

That night I had dinner with the cast and noticed that Jose Ferrer, an extremely macho man, was wearing a small hoop earring. This was 1974, when it wasn't as usual to see a man sporting this adornment as it is today, but I really didn't give the matter much thought. The shooting proceeded smoothly until two days later when I returned to my hotel to be inundated with messages, all marked "urgent," demanding that I phone ABC immediately. When I did, I was greeted by a network executive, who had seen the dailies, yelling in a demented manner, "He's wearing an earring! The man is wearing an goddamn earring! Why is he wearing an earring?!" Thinking quickly, I replied, "He's an angel ... that's his halo." The executive, faced with this situation comedy logic, was immediately mollified and backed down. "Oh, I see, we didn't know that. That makes sense."

The film cut together well and about a month later we heard that it had been picked up to become a series. That's when events took a bizarre turn. Suddenly, Michael Eisner, Barry Diller, and everybody at the network stopped returning my calls. When I tried to get an explanation from studio executives they just looked evasive or at the ground. I was completely baffled because although, over the years, I had seen producers replaced—one came back from lunch to find all the furniture in his office had been removed—it made absolutely no sense to replace me. Even putting aside any thoughts of loyalty or ethics and looking at it purely from a financial point of view, it was stupid and eventually was to cost the studio dearly both in dollars and in the shows I would most likely have gotten on the air. At the time, I had trouble absorbing what was going on and nobody at the studio had the guts or decency to be honest with me. Then I heard that Jose Ferrer had been replaced by Carl Reiner, who was now not only directing but starring in the show, as well as functioning as the executive producer.

I have always had an idealized view of life, believing that if I treated people well they would respond in kind. This trusting, naive way of dealing with life had always stood me in good stead and, at age forty-four, I can honestly say that I had never been treated really badly by anyone. This made the experience all the more painful.

What had happened? I don't know. I didn't know then and I don't know now. My scenario, arrived at through hindsight, is that John Mitchell, an avuncular studio vice president known as a "great salesman" (meaning he had a hearty handshake and tipped head waiters heavily), thought the show needed some extra juice to push it onto the schedule, and had sold me out and promised the network the better-known Carl Reiner as the producer. I don't know how much Carl Reiner had to do with this, but it is curious that he went from being just the director of the pilot to the star, director, and executive producer. It turned out that the show didn't help anyone's career, being canceled after only a few episodes.

I have only rarely lost my temper completely, but this was one of those times, and when I managed to get John Mitchell on the phone I yelled incoherently, ending by saying that the government had put the wrong John Mitchell in jail. Flashing ahead a year, when *Same Time* was nominated for three Tony awards and I was dancing with Jill at the Tony ball, I felt a tap on my shoulder and turned to find John Mitchell. He said, "I just want you to know how terribly proud we all are of you." I said, "Well, I couldn't have done it without you, John." Without any touch of irony, he said, "Thank you."

When it became clear that I had been shafted, I phoned my business manager and told him that he had to get me out of the contract at any price. He said, "No, we're not going to do that. They're in breach of contract. Don't talk to anyone. Just get out of the country." When I started to protest he insisted, so I booked a flight to Hawaii. I never went back to the studio.

A few months later, when I was in rehearsal with the play, I got a call from Murray to tell me that Columbia had agreed to pay me in full for the remaining three years of my contract. I said, "That's nice." He said, "I told you so." I said, "Murray, if you had any class you wouldn't say 'I told you so.'" He responded, "If I had any class I wouldn't have got that settlement!"

On the flight to Hawaii, I took out some airline stationery and started writing the play.

Almost immediately, the characters started to come off the pages. Doris was the easiest—a warm, lovable, decent woman who goes from an uneducated Oakland housewife in the early fifties to a college graduate entrepreneur in the seventies. I have been told I tend to idealize my women characters and Doris was no exception. Although the part of George's wife never appears in the play, we constantly hear about her through stories that are told about her. There is a great deal of Jill, who also returned to university in the sixties as a mature student, in Doris, as there is in most of the women I write. During an intermission of a performance in Boston a woman archly asked Jill, "Which one are you … the mistress or the wife?" Jill said, "I'm both."

With the character of George I wanted to create a quirky, neurotic, charming man who embodied the twentieth-century urban American male. I never base a character solely on anyone I know in real life but often will use the speech rhythms or thought patterns of a friend. In this case, George's quicksilver essence was drawn from the actor Ted Bessell, who later, fortuitously, was in the first replacement cast on Broadway and played it for close to two years.

Plays never really "write themselves," but *Same Time* came close, and by the time we landed in Hawaii I had a rough outline of the first scene. Absolutely transported into my fictitious world, I kept scribbling furiously all through our ten-day vacation at the Mauna Kea Hotel, taking my yellow legal pad and felt-tipped pen onto the beach, to dinner, and even on a catamaran sailing trip. This method of writing longhand started when I first left Canada during a bleak March and arrived in balmy California. Desperate to get the sun, I took to writing by the side of the Chateau Marmont Hotel pool and found it solved a lot of problems. Gregarious by nature, with more the personality of an actor than a writer, I don't like being confined to a room with a typewriter or computer, and can happily work with the TV on and my family around me. Writing amid the swirl of life, I am able to convince myself that I am not missing out on anything.

Since I felt that this would probably be the only play I would ever have the free time to write, I called on all the craft I had assimilated during my years of working in the theater and, because the play leaned towards the use of anecdotes, I packed in almost every funny experience I had ever gone through or witnessed. I was surprised how some of these situations could be adapted and used in a dramatic form. Let me give you an example.

When I first came to Hollywood and Screen Gems, the television arm of Columbia Studios, had expressed interest in signing me to a long-term contract it was decided that it would be a good idea if I met the "brass" of the studio. I was duly ushered into the office of Jackie Cooper, the ex-actor and then president of Screen Gems. Four or five other men in expensive suits were also present. I had only been in Hollywood a few days and was somewhat overwhelmed by the situation but managed to put on a good front and felt I had acquitted myself well for a "kid" from Canada. Then, as

I went to leave, instead of walking out the office door I walked into a clothes closet. Now, that's no big deal. I mean, anybody can do that. The mistake I made was that I stayed in there.

I realize that there's no logical explanation for my doing this, but let me at least try to explain my bizarre behavior. I wasn't sure they had seen me go in, and I thought if I stayed in there for a few minutes until they went to lunch I could sneak out. I was in there for about a minute, with hangers and coats draped around my head, before I realized I'd truly made an ass of myself. When I came out all the men in the room were just staring at me.

Okay, in the play I have George tell about this happening to him after he and a very pregnant Helen had had dinner with some important clients. George comes out of the closet and the sequence continues.

GEORGE ... Okay, it was an embarrassing situation, but I could probably have carried it off. Except for what Helen did. You know what she did?

DORIS What?

GEORGE She peed on the carpet.

DORIS She did *what*?

GEORGE Oh, not right away. First she started to laugh. Tears started to roll down her face. She held her sides. Then she peed all over their Persian carpet. (*Doris is having trouble controlling her laughter.*)

DORIS What did you say?

GEORGE I said, "You'll have to excuse my wife. Ever since her last pregnancy she's had a problem." Then I offered to pay for the cleaning of the carpet.

DORIS Did that help?

GEORGE They said it wasn't necessary. They had a maid. (*Doris is doubled over.*) You think this is funny?

DORIS I've been meaning to tell you ... I just love Helen!

When we returned to LA, I continued to write. Since the events in my plays are always planned before I actually start writing there are no surprises in that area. However, almost every line of dialogue is new to me and a few have popped out that have made me laugh out loud. When that happens I'm filled with an intense desire to hear it before an audience, and if there are enough of these surprises, it usually means I'm on the right track. The first draft (which is basically what we went into rehearsal with) was finished in a month and, with a great deal of trepidation, I gave it to Jill to read, whose opinion I trust the most about my work.

She took it out on the back patio and I tried to keep busy inside the house. Always a good laugher, from time to time I would hear her chuckle. When I sensed that she'd be coming to the end of the play, I watched her through the den window as she finished it and put the script in her lap, with a pensive smile. I went out onto the patio and waited. She said, "I don't know how good this is, but it's exactly the sort of play I like to see when I go to the theater." I believe the second thing she said was, "How come you know so much about adultery?"

I had not had an agent for some time but a few years before had written a play that was represented by Jack Hutto, who, at that time, worked at the William Morris Agency. I had lost touch with him, and the last I had heard was that he had become a travel agent, but, by chance, I bumped into a friend who told me Jack was back in the agency business. I immediately sent him the play, he quickly replied to express his enthusiasm, and, with my blessing, he sent it to three producers with a reading time attached. The three producers were Robert Whitehead, Manny Azenberg, and Morton Gottlieb. The first two rejected it, but Morton immediately committed to a production.

Morton started his career as a publicist working for the legendary Gilbert Miller and then segued into a career as a producer, presenting such plays as *Enter Laughing*, *Sleuth*, and *The Killing of Sister George*. He was, and at this writing still is, given to riding around the streets of New York on a beat-up, rusty bicycle. He claims that the appalling condition of the bike protects it against theft. I believe his well-known reputation as one of the cheapest men in show business is deliberately fostered by such behavior, along with reusing envelopes he has received and being slow on the draw when it comes to picking up checks. His home is furnished with leftover set pieces from his stage productions, including, it is rumored, a coffin from *Special Occasions*, a later flop of mine. Nothing is wasted: his suits are expensively cut clothes acquired from the widows of wealthy dead friends. However, he was fanatically loyal to his backers and carefully watched to see that their investments were not spent on frivolous aspects of production. I don't believe any producers are a hundred percent honest, but in contrast to other producers with whom I have dealt, Morton seems like Abe Lincoln.

When I first met him he had offices in the Palace Theater overlooking Times Square. They were everything I imagined a Broadway theatrical producer's offices should be: musty, cluttered, filled with dusty set models from long-ago productions, old programs, posters, faded pictures, and cracked leather furniture. Nothing like the offices of a film producer. I was back in the theater again and it felt good.

Morton suggested changing the title of the play to *Same Time, Next Year* (I'm still not sure how that comma crept in there) and we talked about the possibility of Gene Saks, who had already read and liked the script, directing the play. Gene had had a distinguished career on Broadway as both an actor and a director. He now lived in LA with his wife Bea Arthur and, after a number of film successes, like Neil Simon's *The Odd Couple*, had recently been involved with the disappointing movie *Mame*, and wanted to get back to the theater.

When I returned to Los Angeles, I met with him at his house where we talked about some minor script changes and made up extensive lists of casting possibilities. Over the next few weeks we were turned down by every one on the lists.

I can't remember all the names we discussed, but I believe Alan Arkin was our first choice for George, with Dick Van Dyke, Alan Alda, Jerry Orbach, and Larry Blyden high on the list. I was very excited about the possibility of Barbara Harris for Doris, but that didn't work out, so we sent the script to Shirley MacLaine but never received any sort of reply. About a week after the opening I was at a movie screening and Shirley approached me in the lobby to gush effusively about how much she enjoyed seeing the play. Bewildered, I blurted out, "But we offered you the play." She said, "I know. Before I could read it I lost the script."

Gene had unique ways of discussing casting. One actor he deemed as "having the wrong-shaped head." When I questioned him about this he explained that "he has a leading man's head. We need a comedy actor's head." He didn't want to consider a certain actress with a background in musical comedy because "I get the feeling that, at any moment, she's about to break into the eleven o'clock number." It was all quite academic anyway, because even actors with the wrong heads were turning us down.

This avalanche of rejections was something I was to experience with all my plays, and the only time I got my first choice was when Jack Lemmon committed to do *Tribute*. Gene was less disturbed than I was by the rejections and surmised that most of the actors who had turned us down had not even seen the script because their agents didn't want their highly paid television and film clients to go to Broadway at much smaller salaries, which meant less commissions for the agents. We decided to circumvent the agents and get the scripts directly to the actors, and in the process learned that Gene had been absolutely correct. We still got a lot of refusals, but at least we knew the actors had seen the script.

I don't remember where the idea for Ellen Burstyn and Charles Grodin originated. I knew something of Chuck's work and had even seen him in the stage play *Tchin Tchin* some years before, so I was happy to go along with the choice. We were both in LA, and I arranged a meeting that took place at his house, where he cooked meatloaf for lunch while wearing a cap he never removed. I discovered later he wore a toupee, which stood us in good stead for the play as we had him gradually go bald as he aged throughout the performance.

We were less familiar with Ellen's work, but she was currently in the film *Alice Doesn't Live Here Anymore*, for which she was later to win an Oscar, so Gene and I went to see the film. I felt that her open, Irish face and common touch were ideal for the role of Doris and afterwards, while walking up Westwood Boulevard, I kept pushing to cast her (at this point I would have pushed to cast *anybody*), but Gene's reaction was muted. When I asked him what the problem was he grimaced and said, "I don't know. There's something about her that's a pain in the ass." These words would come back to me many times during the next few weeks.

We arranged for the four of us to meet in New York for an "unofficial" reading of the play two weeks before rehearsals were due to start. We felt that this would give me time to do any small rewrites I thought necessary before we plunged into rehearsals. Gene kept saying that he didn't want to "go in the hole" financially so was staying at a dreary hotel in midtown Manhattan, and it was in his depressing room where the reading took place.

Now, it is generally thought that the most traumatic experience for a playwright is the opening night performance. Although this does contain its own share of horrors, for me, it runs a poor second to the first time I hear my play read. This is when I find out if the play hangs together and makes any sense at all or whether all the work done over the past year has been a total waste of time and effort. As usual, the awkward small talk that precedes a reading took place. The one unusual aspect of this was that Ellen told us she had an ex-husband named Neil Burstyn, who had suffered from drug use and was presently in an institution but was about to be released and could cause some problems. Gene and I didn't really pay much attention to this story, dismissing it as the typical exaggeration of an actress.

The two began to read and slowly my sphincter relaxed as I realized the play was not complete nonsense. I soon found myself smiling and even laughing out loud, something I almost never do when watching my own work, preferring to bury my head in my hands and remain completely silent. This behavior is sometimes hard on actors who, understandably, want a vocal reaction to their performance. The truth is that the playwright is not concentrating on their reading but is listening to his play and realizing, "My God they're going to say this rubbish out loud and everybody is going to hear." Having said that, Charles Grodin is about the only actor who made me laugh above and beyond the lines. Sometimes he went too *far* beyond and above, but when he was restrained his off-beat delivery and comic paranoia always got to me.

At the end of the reading I felt light-headedly optimistic, believing the only work for me to do on the play was some minor cutting. I wouldn't have felt so lighthearted if I'd known that the next time I would hear my play in full, without interruption, would be five weeks later. Until then I'd be working from the memory of this first reading. We arranged to meet the next day, this time in my suite at the Sherry Netherland, to hear some comments Ellen wanted to make.

I expected some general remarks about the play, with perhaps a few questions about her character. This fantasy was shattered when, without even opening the script, Ellen said, "About the title."

Ellen Burnstyn and Charles
Grodin—*Same Time, Next Year.*
PHOTO: MARTHA SWOPE

The morning after the opening
night. Producer Morton Gottlieb
serving coffee to the eager ticket
buyers.

The New York set for *Same Time, Next Year,* designed by Bill Ritman, which was
copied all over the world. PHOTO: MARTHA SWOPE.

Anthony Perkins and Mia Farrow in *Romantic Comedy* on Broadway.

PHOTO: MARTHA SWOPE.

I Remember You in Budapest.

I Remember You in Budapest.

Jack Lemmon in *Tribute*.

Jean Pierre Cassel and Anny
Duperay in the Paris production of
Romantic Comedy, retitled *La Fille sur
La Banquette Arriere.*

My name up in lights on
Shaftesbury Avenue.

Jan Waters and John Alderton in the London production of *Special Occasions*. PHOTO: ZOË DOMINIC.

Richard Mulligan and Suzanne Pleschette in the Broadway production of *Special Occasions*. PHOTO: MARTHA SWOPE.

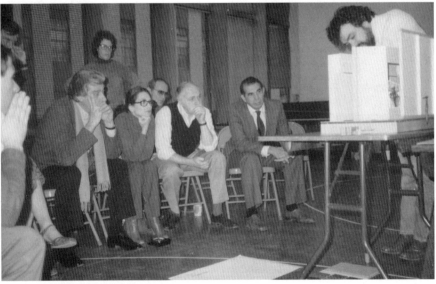

David Jenkins explaining the multiple sets of *Special Occasions* to Richard Mulligan, Suzanne Pleschette, Gene Saks, and Morton Gottlieb. They had good reasons to look worried.

Susannah York and Dennis Quilley in the London production of *Fatal Attraction*. PHOTO: ZOË DOMINIC.

Same Time, Next Year at the Anton Chekhov Theatre in Moscow.

Ken Howard on the Toronto set of *Fatal Attraction*.

Musical of *Same Time, Next Year* (retitled *Every Time I See You*) in Budapest.

At the Palaise Royal Theatre in Paris where *Romantic Comedy* was renamed *The Girl In the Back Seat*.

Directing Nancy Dussault and Tom Troupe in *Same Time Another Year* at the Pasadena Playhouse. PHOTO BY CRAIG SCHWARTZ.

Paula Wilcox and Denis Waterman in the British production of *Same Time Another Year*, 1999.

Westport Playhouse: checking to see that my name is spelled right in the program.

Return Engagements in summer stock. David Hedison, Louise Sorrel, and Tom Troupe.

This was the beginning of perhaps the worst day of my career in show business. She attacked every line, not so much on any basis of logic, but whether it jibed with her personal philosophy. When she wasn't doing this she was telling me about all the lines and attitudes that weren't funny. Now, one of the problems with discussing comedy is that once you have to explain *why* something is funny you've lost the debate. This situation is made even more difficult when the person you're trying to convince has a poor sense of humor. Ellen may have a sense of humor, but you'd need Sherlock Holmes to find it.

At this point in my career I had appeared in over a hundred comedies by the best writers in the world, and had written two stage comedies, fifteen one-hour TV comedies, and close to a hundred television comedy episodes, so when it came down to judging whether an audience would laugh I was on very solid ground. This is not to say I believed everything I wrote was written in stone. In fact, over the years, I have worked with hundreds of actors who, I believe, would agree that I'm quite willing to change the text if I feel the requests are reasonable. However, I will also fiercely protect material I believe in. This was fortunate in this case because some of the speeches Ellen wanted to cut turned out to get the biggest laughs in the play. Of course, when these passages were validated by an audience with huge laughs, I never heard another word from her, but until then it was a tiresome battle.

I've since tried to rationalize our mutual antagonism with the thought that it was a case of her overstating and my habit of understating. But perhaps a more accurate reason might be that Ellen, who had worked under a couple of different names in the past, did not really become well known until she was in her forties, and I've observed that actors who have suffered decades of a lack of recognition sometimes become willful and misuse their power when they do become stars. I'm sorry we didn't become friends, as I did admire her talent and still do.

Our main problem was that Ellen had just discovered the women's movement and treated me as if I was a combination of Attila the Hun and John Wayne. In fact, I felt I knew more about feminism than she did and had even written a television play way back in 1957 and a feature film in the sixties that, although awful in execution, explored the subject and was well intentioned. More to the point, the character of Doris was written to progress through an arc that began when she was an uneducated housewife in Oakland in 1953 and ended when she had developed into a successful woman with a raised consciousness some twenty-four years later. Gene absorbs a play rather slowly so the exchanges, growing more heated as the day progressed, were all between Ellen and me. At one point she yelled, "If someone said that to me I'd tell him to cut off his cock and stuff it into his mouth!" She then stormed into the kitchenette a few feet away, from where we heard sounds of sobbing. Well, it's hard to imagine her sobbing but she sure was making a hell of a racket.

Gene, Chuck, and I, three grown men, were left sitting in stunned silence contemplating the carpet. There was a long pause before Gene, his brow furrowed, leaned forward and said, "Did she tell you to cut off your cock and stuff it into your mouth?" I said, "No, I don't think so. I think she said if *someone* said that to her she'd tell *him* to cut off his cock and stuff it into *his* mouth." Gene said, "No, I think she told you to do it, Bern." Chuck, coming over to our side for the first time, said, "I don't think she should have told you to do that. That was unnecessary." "No," I repeated. "It was the character she was talking about." The other two looked dubious, then the three of us lapsed into silence, each contemplating the ceiling, the walls, or the blank TV screen as Ellen completed her tantrum.

At this point, Ellen, clear-eyed and as cheerful as she can ever get, reentered the room and launched into some further notes as if nothing untoward had happened.

Shortly after, as soon as she and Chuck had left, I turned to Gene and said, "Look, I didn't get out of television for this. Let's get rid of her." He agreed that this would be a wonderful idea but pointed out that she had a run of the play contract. "What does that mean?" I asked. He said, "It means that however long the play runs, she will have to be paid full salary." Oh well, nobody said it would be easy.

During the next two weeks I did a major rewrite of the second scene in the first act, which was originally about sexual jealousy but became about George's guilt. This came about because Chuck (who apparently had just realized that the play dealt with adultery) kept harping about the morality of the piece with the oft-repeated line, "I can hear the audience leaving in droves." The play was long and the new material did help reduce the length, but it's my least favorite scene, and I would usually creep out of the theater and have a smoke when it was being played. Of course, I couldn't do this when I later appeared in the play myself, but I always had the urge to address the audience and invite them all outside for a cigarette.

Two weeks later, on a damp February morning, I showed up at the New Amsterdam Theater for the first day of rehearsals.

★ Next day on your dressing room they pin a star ★

★
The New Amsterdam Theater is on Forty-Second Street and once housed the Ziegfeld Follies but had long since degenerated into a pornographic movie house. Our rehearsals were to take place in a small theater up under the roof, where Al Jolson had performed his famous midnight shows. It was reached by a rickety, anxiety-inducing elevator, and the theater itself had a small stage and some absolutely filthy, cobwebbed seats; the outside could only be glimpsed through soot-encrusted skylights. It was also freezing cold. It seemed to me the room was more conducive to rehearsing *Oliver Twist* than a light, romantic comedy. The atmosphere was made even more depressing by Chuck and Ellen insisting that we have a "closed rehearsal," which meant that, besides themselves, only Gene, myself, and Warren Crane, our stage manager, were present. Thank God for Warren, a level-headed professional, who was to stage manage many plays of mine in the future.

My usual rehearsal routine is that I am present for the first read-through and then make myself scarce for about ten days while the actors stumble through the blocking and feel free to make all their mistakes in private. During this period, if I like the people in the cast personally, which I usually do, I will often drop in for lunch so that I keep connected with the production. However, I used this time during the *Same Time* rehearsals to scour the city for spoken word and nostalgia records to put together tapes that were emblematic of the times to play between the scenes. They also served to give the actors twenty to thirty seconds to make the fast changes required but, more importantly, underscored the events of the past thirty years. The added bonus was that the tapes had a tremendous emotional effect on the audience as they were reminded of the times they had lived through.

Before the stop-and-start reading, Chuck surprised us with the thought that the two should have almost no physical contact on stage because "There's no point in rubbing people's noses in it." He obviously could hear "the audience leaving in droves." Even Ellen was baffled by this theory, and we secretly referred to Chuck as "the Reverend Davidson." After the reading, which included the new second scene and held no surprises, I escaped the frigid room onto the crowded pavements of Forty-Second Street where, compared to the dismal atmosphere inside, the assorted pimps, hookers, drug pushers, and derelicts seemed positively festive.

The next time I attended rehearsals I was hoping to see the rough shape of some of the scenes that would at least give me the feel of the play. What I did see were two actors reading about three lines before launching into endless, convoluted discussions about perfectly obvious matters that could have been explained in about three seconds. This tedious behavior went on for hours, with my entire body becoming clenched as my sunny little comedy was reduced to the sort of indulgent, dreary exercise often seen in acting classes.

The following days were no better. Chuck had an aversion to using props and, even though there was a phone on the set, would pantomime picking it up. When I whispered to Gene, "Why doesn't he pick up the phone?" he said, "It's called an actor not committing." He would also mime getting dressed rather than using the costumes laid out, and the following exchanges would take place.

GENE Chuck, would you please use the pants?

CHUCK I know how to put on a pair of pants.

GENE We need to time the sequence, Chuck.

CHUCK I put my pants on every morning.

And so it went. A curtain sequence where a glass breaks in his hand was abandoned because he couldn't or wouldn't handle it. Actors who later replaced him using the same blocking would comment that the character of George never touched anything on the set ... including the leading lady.

Ellen, on the other hand, *loved* props. In one scene, when she was energetically brushing her hair, I pointed out to Gene that she was going to be wearing wigs. He wearily said, "I know."

It was about this time that Neil Burstyn, Ellen's ex-husband, got into the rehearsal hall. Nobody seems to know how he managed to find out where we were working, but his intrusion added a bizarre element to the proceedings. I was not present when he appeared, but I gather Morton and other assorted people from the production office were summoned to reason with him before managing to usher him out. Chuck nervously asked Ellen, "If he got into the theater would he do me any harm?" Ellen thought for a moment too long and slowly said, "Oh, I don't ... *think* so."

This didn't reassure him at all, and when I was at rehearsals later that day the following scene took place:

CHUCK (*from the script*) Look, I know how you feel. I wouldn't even suggest it if ... (*He stops, turns to Gene out front*) I'm sorry, I just can't concentrate with ...

GENE Just go on, Chuck.

CHUCK (*starting again*) Look, I know how you feel. I wouldn't even ... (*He stops again*) Is everybody here? I just saw a flash of something go past that door.

GENE It was Warren, Chuck. He went to the bathroom.

CHUCK Oh, okay … I just … well … this is difficult … (*He starts again*) Look, I know how you feel. I wouldn't even suggest it if … (*He stops*) What color sweater was he wearing? I saw a flash of orange.

GENE (*to me*) What color is Warren's sweater?

ME Orange.

CHUCK Oh. You know, this isn't easy.

I still hadn't seen anything like a run-through of my play, and what I had seen was lifeless and awkward, but I was hoping that our first run-through on the Wednesday before we departed for Boston on Friday would lift my spirits. We had invited a small group of people connected with the production, so it would be the first time that the play was performed before any kind of audience, and I was praying that this would bring the comedy alive. It didn't. The run-through was a disaster. Ragged, deadly dull, and if I had been the producer, I would have been tempted to close the show before it opened. Morton Gottlieb was unfailingly optimistic (one of his greatest strengths) and predicted that the final run-through the next day would be much better. But there was no run-through the next day because Chuck had a sore throat and begged off.

The following morning, Morton, Jill, and I, all lovers of theatrical tradition, boarded the train in a blinding snowstorm for the journey to Boston in an attempt to re-create the old days when playwrights and producers traveled by rail to out-of-town theaters. On the way, Morton told me that Neil Burstyn had broken into Ellen's house the night before but that everything would be okay because he had been put back in the institution. This was a well-intentioned lie.

We all checked into the Copley Plaza Hotel and I hurried through the slush to the Colonial Theater, which was some ten blocks away. On entering this beautiful red plush and marble old

Victorian-style theater, my eyes immediately went to the charming, intimate set designed by Bill Ritman and later duplicated all over the world. It was perfect. I moved down the aisle to take a closer look and noticed Chuck moving slowly along the raised partition that divided the orchestra pit from the audience. When I asked what he was doing, he said he was pacing off the distance to see how long he had to get off the stage should Neil Burstyn get into the theater. I told him that Neil was back in the institution, which, understandably, relieved his mind.

We then had a technical rehearsal, which I normally enjoy, as I find it soothing to sit in a darkened theater and watch a play physically come to life with no performances to worry about. This time, though, I was anxious to get to the dress rehearsal. Maybe I'd finally see my play. Not yet. The costumes by Jane Greenwood helped, but the performances still looked awfully rough to me, and I trudged back to the Copley dreading the Saturday matinee the next day. Chuck and Ellen wanted to cancel the performance, but too many tickets had been sold and Morton insisted that they play.

The next morning before I left for the theater Jill, who had decided to skip the first performance and see it that night, gave me an inexpensive poster she had bought. It was a picture of a turtle, with the caption, "Behold the turtle who only makes progress when he sticks his neck out." Corny but comforting. I still have it ... one of the few artifacts that survived a fire that later destroyed almost all our belongings.

After a quick visit backstage to see Ellen and Chuck, who nervously repeated a refrain I'd been hearing for days about him "being a money player" who came through on first performances, I wended my way through the full house to stand behind the orchestra section, where I could watch the show. This position would be a favorite of mine for years to come as I've never been able to see any play I've written while sitting down. Sometimes I even have to fight the urge to dart around and tell audience members, "It gets better, it gets better!" When I'm not standing at the back of the theater, I can usually be found backstage listening to the dialogue over the Tannoy speakers, protected from the possibility of hearing any audience member say anything negative about the play.

The curtain went up and I fell into the time-honored ritual of the playwright helping to wear out the theater carpet. I hadn't read Moss Hart's *Act One* for nothing. Back and forth, back and forth. Then, on the second "forth," I was brought to a sudden halt by a laugh. A big laugh. This was immediately followed by an explosive laugh, then another, and another. I stared unbelievingly at the stage. It wasn't that the laughs weren't coming where I'd planned but that they were so enormous. The laughter kept building throughout the act until it verged on hysteria and, at one point, the audience seemed out of control. It crossed my mind that this might be some kind of freak audience. Was there an Ellen Burstyn cult in Boston?

The laughter didn't diminish during the second act, but I still didn't fully believe that this was a "normal" reaction, and when I phoned Jill at the hotel I played it very cool, saying that I wanted to reserve judgment until I saw it again that night in front of another audience. Inside me, though, something was screaming, "*Holy shit*!!!" Or words to that effect.

The reaction that night was equally enthusiastic and I was able to tell myself that at least I'd written a play that made an audience laugh. Perhaps even more gratifying was that during the serious moments the house had gone dead silent.

Morton was optimistic but said, "Let's hope the reviews on Monday are good." Reviews? I thought we were in Boston for a try-out, an extension of the rehearsal period during which we could fix anything that needed it. I learned that not only were the notices important for business in Boston but, because we had almost no ticket sales in New York, it was crucial that any advance word on Broadway be good.

The performance on Monday went well and we all stayed up at the bar in the Copley to wait for the reviews ... really a mini-Broadway opening. Eliot Norton, the dean of Boston critics, gave us a flat-out rave, and although Kevin Kelly, the other important reviewer, quibbled with some aspects, it was what is called a "good business" notice. Both the *Christian Science Monitor* and national *Variety* were excellent, and I went to bed with my confidence in the play restored. This didn't mean that I believed the play would be a hit in New York, but it did bolster my modest hopes that it might run for maybe a month on Broadway and do quite well in summer stock.

The only work I did on the play in Boston was to change one curtain line. Chuck thought the line made him "unsympathetic" and couldn't or wouldn't play it properly. I thought that it was important he feel comfortable and offered to change the line, but Gene refused, saying that the original line was perfect. A brilliant actor, Gene then demonstrated how it should be played. I pointed out that *he* could play it but Chuck couldn't and, in a complete reversal of the director pushing the playwright to rewrite the text, badgered him into letting me change it. He finally gave in.

Word of mouth spread rapidly. We were completely sold out and the show was "playing like a hit." Everything seemed perfect. Then, when I returned to my hotel one day, I picked up a number of urgent messages from Chuck that I see him right away. Now, to understand the following situation you should know that in each scene the characters tell two stories, one good and one bad, about their respective spouses Helen and Harry. At the end of the play the audience should feel they know George's wife, Helen, and Doris's husband, Harry, well, even though they never appear on stage. When I got to Chuck's dressing room, which was always so neat a surgeon could have operated in it, and which for some reason was kept at the temperature of a hothouse, I was greeted by a grim expression and the flat statement, "We're in a lot of trouble." When I asked why he said, "The audience likes Helen better than they do me." Mystified, I said, "She's not in the play, Chuck." He said, "I know, but every time I tell a story about her they go crazy. If they like her that much they must hate me." After taking a moment to make sure he wasn't putting me on, I said, "What do you want me to do about it?" He said, "Write a story putting her in a bad light." He quickly added, "Don't make it funny, just make her look bad." I still couldn't believe what I was hearing … an actor competing with an offstage character. I said, "Look, I'll do it if she gets a Tony nomination for best supporting actress." He didn't smile.

Oddly enough, I once worked with an actor who was in competition with *himself*. My first job in Hollywood was on a show that starred Bob Cummings, who loved to play not only himself but his own grandfather on the show. One day we rehearsed a setup where Bob, as himself, had a line and then Bob, as his grandfather, had a line, which got a laugh before an exit. We were all ready to shoot when Bob said, "Wait a minute … I'm the star of the show. Why is *he* getting the laugh?" The director said, "But you are him, Bob." Bob said, "I think me as me should get the laugh, not me as him." And that's the way it was shot.

To be fair to Chuck, it's not only the actors who get a little crazy when they're out of town with a play. One night, I took some time off and didn't watch the performance. Afterwards, while having a drink with Gene, he casually remarked, "Someone in the theater tonight threw up." Panic stricken, I immediately asked, "On what line?" He looked at me as one might regard a slightly dim child and gently explained that it probably had more to do with something the person had eaten than something I'd written.

Another night, during a performance, I saw a woman get out of her seat and start to wander around the side aisles and the back of the theater. Quite uncharacteristically, I grabbed her by the arm and hissed, "Will you sit down, you're missing the best part!" She looked at me: it was Tharon Musser, our lighting designer, who had been checking the lights.

Our daughter, Laurie, who was then a student at Sarah Lawrence College, arrived in Boston desperate to see the play. She had a temperature of over a hundred, a runny nose, runny eyes, and a hacking cough. I told her that there was no way she was going to see the play in that condition. She pleaded with me and claims I said, "Okay, you can go, but if you have to cough ... cough while the audience is laughing!"

My new agent, Jack Hutto, came to Boston, and after he'd been there for about three days I asked him how he could spend so much time away from his other clients. He said he didn't have any other clients and went on to tell me that if my play wasn't a success he would have to get out of show business again. Nothing like a little extra pressure to make my day. A week after the play opened I called him in New York, to be told that "he was on holiday in the south of France!"

By now I had been away from home for over two months, and was anxious to get the Broadway opening over with and go home to California and my family and friends. On March 9, I moved back to New York and into the Sherry Netherland Hotel to get ready for our March 13 opening.

At about this time I got a preproduction movie offer for the play. It was for three hundred thousand dollars, with the price going up the longer the play ran. It was low even for 1975 but would certainly have given me a cushion of cash should the play fail. I turned it down, mostly because my brain was too numb to absorb the offer but also because of a feeling that if I'd come this far, I may as well go for broke. The play eventually sold for a million plus an unheard of ten percent of the gross.

Our schedule was to play only four previews before opening on Thursday the thirteenth. The reaction to the first preview was way down from any performance we'd had in Boston, but we felt this was due to the cast adjusting to the Brooks Atkinson Theater, which was two-thirds the size of the Colonial in Boston, with correspondingly diminished laughter. The second preview was only slightly better and I began to get the panicky feeling that the Boston experience was a complete fluke. Two friends, the novelist Arthur Hailey and his wife, Sheila, attended the Wednesday matinee performance and have since told me that they encountered me on Forty-Seventh Street, gray, with eyes circled in black like a raccoon. I told them it was all a "disaster." This mystified them as they felt they had just left a performance with "hit" written all over it. I have no memory of this exchange, but then I have little memory of that week at all.

Then, after the matinee performance, Neil Burstyn was spotted buying a ticket for that evening's performance. This event was kept from me.

Morton was now faced with a dilemma: legally he couldn't bar Neil Burstyn from the theater, although he knew his presence could be disruptive. On the other hand, he preferred that he see the last preview performance rather than possibly ruin the opening night. He chose to recruit some very tall basketball players and put them in seats around Neil (pity the poor people behind them) in case he started to cause a disturbance. Some time during the first act, Neil started to loudly talk to the stage. Ellen recognized the voice, and Chuck could see by her expression that she had recognized him and probably thought he was going to be shot. Warren Crane, the stage manager, said that from that point on the performances went completely to pieces. At the intermission, when they hustled Neil out, he said that "he was underrehearsed and would be better on opening night."

I had overdosed on the play by then and wasn't at this performance, but when Gene related what had happened I blurted out, "My God, what if he gets in tomorrow night?!" Gene said, "Oh, I think the critics would lean over backwards. …" This was of no comfort to me at all as I grappled with the fact that my first Broadway opening could be ruined by a crazed ex-husband.

Ellen managed to produce a photo of Neil, which was distributed to the front of the house staff, and some security guards were hired. As soon as Ellen came through the stage door, it was securely locked. All this time, Neil was seated across the street, in front of the Biltmore Theater, watching the proceedings. Some months later, I heard that he had died.

On opening night I dropped by the theater to distribute gifts to the cast and crew. While I was doing this, Jill, our son, Christopher, and our daughter, Laurie, were all getting dressed in one room together. This was the first time in years (if ever) that they'd all dressed together, and Jill said that the two women pulling on panty hose and Chris struggling with an almost-never-worn blue suit reminded her of three gladiators preparing to enter the arena to do battle.

As soon as the curtain went up, I returned to the hotel to wash my hair, play my harmonica, and wait to see whether my life would be changed.

★ The movie, the musical, and laughs in other languages ★

A friend of mine once said that I was the only playwright he knew who drove a Bentley *before* his first Broadway hit. It wasn't that I was "to the manor born" (far from it), but it was true that my income from the years of writing television had earned my family a comfortable existence that included a two-acre estate in Brentwood with a swimming pool and tennis court, so the success of *Same Time* did not change our lives in any material way. It did, however, change my life in a more profound manner because, apart from the financial independence it gave me to continue working in the uncertain business of the theater, it gave me the confidence to start "working without a net" and risk failure.

I have often heard successful people when asked whether they learned more from success or failure answer "failure." I don't quite understand this; everybody has failures—that's easy to get—but success is rare and helps you to work without the *fear* of failure and take the chance of falling flat on your face … or exceeding your grasp.

After the play opened I was given some advice to take time to savor the success and not to immediately start on another play. This made sense to me, so, although I had an idea for another play, whenever I felt like putting something on paper, I went to lunch or worked on my tennis forehand.

I didn't return to New York until the Tony Awards. Ellen, Gene, and I were nominated (the play had already won the Drama Desk Award), but Chuck was overlooked, which I thought was unfair as he was the one who had provided the energy and performance that drove the play. The role of George is infinitely more difficult to play than the part of Doris, but this lack of recognition became a pattern in later productions. The woman always got the best notices, and when my wife and I subsequently played the parts I, only half-jokingly, put a statement in the program announcing that the woman always got the best reviews. On the day the nominations were announced, Chuck, to his credit, was discovered in bed on the set wearing a black armband.

Ellen won the Tony for Best Actress and in her speech acknowledged Chuck's contribution. She did not mention Gene, Morton, me, or anybody else.

The next time I went to New York was when Chuck and Ellen were leaving after a ten-month stint, and Joyce Van Patten and Conrad Janis were replacing them. Morton had planned a small good-bye party combined with a welcoming party for the new cast. Chuck and Ellen chose not to attend and I had the feeling that they really thought the play would close as soon as they left. It was planned that Joyce and Conrad would play in New York for six weeks before going out with the national touring company. Their Broadway roles would be filled by Loretta Swit and Ted Bessell. Another company featuring Barbara Rush and Tom Troupe was also out on the road, so I had three American companies playing simultaneously.

A London production was also being planned and I flew to England to help set it up. Eric Thompson, a well-known British director, later also known as the father of the actress Emma Thompson, was already signed for the show. I found him to be a congenial man and we got along well. After a couple of days of casting meetings, it was decided to offer the play to an actor named Michael Crawford, who had just come off an enormously popular TV situation comedy and was currently starring in the West End musical, *Billy Liar*. I would have preferred a more prestigious legitimate actor, but, at this point, I had just finished helping cast three American companies and was tired of the whole process, so when it was pointed out that with Michael Crawford we could sell out the huge Prince of Wales Theatre, I agreed. It was then arranged for me to meet him.

Now, this was pre-*Phantom of the Opera* and I had no idea what he looked like. Our meeting place was in a dimly lit restaurant. I arrived first, and shortly after, a tall red-haired man joined me at my table and started to talk about "Michael." It went something like this: "When they come to see Michael they expect to see ..." or "Michael's audience likes to see him in a play that ..." etc. I assumed that this must be Michael's agent. This discussion of Michael's talent and appeal went on for about half an hour before I looked around and said, "Where *is* Michael?" He said, "*I'm* Michael."

The play ran for a year, so I guess everyone else knew who Michael was. I never did see the production but was told there were a lot of emotional offstage scenes connected with the play. These were brought about because Frances Cuka, the actress playing Doris, got better reviews than Michael. Big surprise.

I did see the Paris production, *Même heure l'année prochaine*, which I found charming. It ran for four years, starring Jean Piat and Nicole Courcel. I also visited the Spanish production and before the show met with the producer, who told me that they did two performances a night, seven nights a week. I said, "My God, don't the actors get tired?" He said, "Don't tell them." This was a strange production because the leading man had a Castilian lisp and the leading woman was so old (or so tired from fourteen performances a week) that I was sure the last scene would take place in the graveyard. It also ran for four years.

Productions were springing up like McDonald's franchises all over the world and, because in those days the writer received ten percent of the box office gross, I was finally beginning to believe that I really *wouldn't* have to endure any more network story conferences. The backers were pretty happy too because, although the Broadway production was capitalized at $230,000, it came into town for $175,000 and their initial investment was returned within weeks. It is hard to imagine with today's inflated prices that our top ticket was $14, our capacity about $72,000, and our breakeven $37,000.

I have never invested money in any of my plays, and when Jill suggested we put a modest amount into *Same Time*, I reminded her that we had been financially wiped out when we were twenty-four and produced a season of twenty-five plays at a summer theater. It may have been "character building," but I still had the psychic scars and prematurely gray hair. Without telling me, she bought a half share for our two children, who still receive dividend checks from their theatrical investments. I say investments, plural, because I later learned that they had taken their "winnings" from *Same Time* and put them into my next play, *Tribute*, and then taken those profits and put them into *Romantic Comedy*. Curiously (and somewhat suspiciously) they did not invest in my next play *Special Occasions*, which ran for one night on Broadway. When I asked whether their lack of confidence in the project had anything to do with the script, they protested that this wasn't a factor; they just thought that expecting more than three hits in a row was asking too much. I still haven't figured out whether they were smart or just lucky.

I didn't want the pressure of any of my friends having money in the play and I only let one, the actor Dick Van Patten, invest. This was because Dick is an inveterate gambler, and I figured if he didn't put it in my play he'd only put it on a horse. *Same Time* won "going away."

I first met Dick because of our mutual passion for tennis, not through show business. Some thirty years ago he phoned to tell me that he had heard of the tennis prowess of my son, Christopher, and wanted to know if he'd be interested in becoming the doubles partner of his son Vincent, who was already making a name for himself on the junior tennis circuit. Vincent went on to have a successful career in world-class tennis but eventually joined the "family business" of show business as an actor. By then Dick and I had forged our own friendship.

Dick had been an enormously successful child actor before appearing in twenty-seven Broadway plays and starring in the TV series *Eight Is Enough*, and a great deal of the wonder and enthusiasm that is the stock in trade of kid performers still clings to him, which people find irresistible. He is rarely out of work but finds time to indulge in such diverse passions as ocean swimming—the colder the better—gambling (don't be fooled by that choirmaster appearance—he'll kill you at the poker table), horse racing, tennis, theater, professional boxing, and circus freaks. I'm not even going to try to explain that last one.

The Van Pattens live in a charming, rambling bungalow in the San Fernando Valley, but playing tennis on their court is rather like playing in the middle of Times Square. There is always music—pop songs from the forties and fifties—blaring forth on an outside speaker, the courtside phone is always ringing, a variety of small grandchildren wander through the garden, along with an assortment of racetrack habitués, actors, bikini-clad *Baywatch* girls, fighters, celebrities showing up for tennis lessons from Dick's son Nils, publicity men, agents, and the odd circus freak. It certainly hones one's concentration.

Dick has an offbeat sense of logic. One day he joined Laurie and Christopher in our kitchen for some ice cream. While enthusiastically spooning it onto a plate, he said, "You know why only intelligent people like ice cream?" Our kids were nonplussed. He said, "Because it tastes so good you'd have to be *stupid* not to like it!"

His sister Joyce is also a well-known actor and I was happy to have her in the Broadway and national company of *Same Time, Next Year*. Not long ago Dick was hired to play Cap'n Andy in the Chicago company of *Showboat*, and when the actress playing his wife left the cast, Dick enthusiastically (always) suggested that Joyce replace her. Only Dick would suggest that his sister play his wife. And she did.

About two years after the Broadway opening, Jill and I were asked by John Neville, who was the artistic director of the Citadel Theatre in Edmonton, to appear in the play there. I was reluctant to return to acting after a twenty-year hiatus, but Jill felt that since we had appeared in another two-character play, *The Fourposter*, when we were young, this would nicely complete the circle.

Carol Burnett and Dick Van Dyke were helping to fill the Huntington Hartford (since then rechristened the Doolittle) Theater in Hollywood, so, with Warren Crane directing, we had the luxury of rehearsing on their set. The word "fuck" is used only once in the play, but Carol felt uncomfortable saying it and changed the word to "hump," which I felt was much more offensive and used to kid her about. When Jill and I opened in the play she sent us a telegram that read: "Have a good time and for heaven's sake don't hump it up!"

I had met Dick Van Dyke once before, but, fortunately, I don't believe he remembered the encounter. A new arrival in Los Angeles, I was having lunch in the crowded cafeteria at CBS on Fairfax Avenue. Dick came in and took the only seat available, which happened to be next to mine. Uncharacteristically (I'm really very shy) I blurted out that I was a big fan of his. He graciously murmured his thanks and I took a gulp of the hot chocolate I was drinking, which was the kind that had small marshmallows floating on top. Dick suddenly turned to me and said, "And what do you do?" I swallowed the drink the wrong way and as I looked at him I realized I had marshmallows coming out of my nose. Dick regarded me gravely for a moment, indicated my nose, and said, "You know, not many people can do that."

After two weeks of rehearsal in LA, with our son, Christopher, in tow, who was going to get his theatrical feet wet as an assistant stage manager, we left for Canada. Chris cleverly had his experience classified as a senior class project, and although it proved useful in some respects (he learned to make a bed in ten seconds flat), he didn't get infected by the theater bug and eventually became a writer and magazine editor. I remember at one point between scenes, when I thought my throat was closing up, I yelled at him to get me some water. He was rushing around completing his chores and yelled back, "I'm not allowed to talk to the star!"

Edmonton is not a city that anyone is going to write a song about ... especially in March ... and in 1977 was not overflowing with luxury hotels. The Citadel Theatre itself was beautiful, so the city was not a complete cultural backwater, but I must admit I felt great trepidation when, just before our first preview, I noticed that almost every car in the audience parking lot had a kayak strapped to its roof. After changing our accommodation twice, we accepted the fact that the most comfortable place in town was our dressing room at the theater, where I spent an inordinate amount of time in the shower trying to get the dye out of my hair after each performance. I had envisioned spending my days polishing my new play, *Tribute*, and acting at night, but I immediately regressed to the persona of an actor ("My throat's sore and nobody cares!") with my whole day geared towards the performance that night. Unprepared for the rigors of eight performances a week, I barely looked at the new script. I remember that early in the run I was so tired I went fast asleep while sitting up in front of my dressing-room mirror. Of course, all those showers could have sapped my strength. I had always grumbled about actors who would only stay with a play for a limited time, and Jill now suggested that in the future I might be more sympathetic to this "on-the-job fatigue."

I have always been a quick study and, since I wrote the piece, didn't spend a great deal of time studying the lines. During the previews our director, Warren Crane, who by this time had directed a number of companies, told me that he always made a speech to the cast that because I wrote with a certain rhythm not a word could be changed and paraphrasing was completely unacceptable. I asked him why he was telling me this. He said, "Because you're paraphrasing." A piece of paper noting every paraphrase was delivered to my dressing room after the next three performances.

After the dress rehearsal, while giving notes, Warren casually said, "Bern, the last few rows can see your bald spot. Better get someone to brown it in." I turned to Jill, "Do I have a bald spot?" She made a sympathetic face. "I wasn't going to tell you."

There were other problems involving makeup. When I was a young actor I was mostly cast in character roles and was always trying to look older than I was with the use of mustaches, white hair, and painted-on wrinkles. Now my problem, at least in the early part of the play, was to look younger, but I did not take into account that, in the twenty years since I'd appeared on stage, lighting techniques had changed. In an effort to recapture my youth I'm afraid I went a little heavy on the blue eye shadow. Our daughter, Laurie, who by now knew the play very well, flew up to see us and, after the show, came backstage to tell us how wonderful we were. I asked her if she had any negative notes. She said, "Well, your eye makeup's a little heavy, Daddy." I said, "How heavy?" She said, "Well, it looks as if you're about to dance *Swan Lake*." When I asked her where she was sitting she told me she was standing at the back of the theater. It was a very large theater, so the Max Factor stock must have really gone up that week.

The production was a big success with, of course, Jill getting better reviews than I, but after the opening night I really wanted to go home because I realized that there were many other people who could act this role better but only I could have written it, and my place was not on stage but behind a yellow legal pad. The relationship between two actors, even when they're married, or perhaps especially if they're married, playing in a two-character piece can be fraught, but we had only one small frisson. Since I was the author of the play we had made a pact that we would not give each other acting notes. In other words, no "Are you really going to play it that way?" questions. So far we'd stuck to the agreement. Now, at one point the character of Doris has to burst into peals of laughter, which is much more difficult to do than to cry on stage. Jill happens to be sensational at laughing on stage. The audience loved the way she laughed. The critics mentioned how well she laughed. One night, between scenes, during our frantic offstage quick change, I said, "Don't you think the laughing's getting a bit much?" She said, "No." The next night she was laughing so hard she forgot her lines. After the show I thought I was remarkably restrained when I pointed out that the scene was about a man's son dying, not a woman laughing. She concurred and that was the extent of our disagreement.

I had heard the expression "trapped in a hit" and this was the situation in which we found ourselves. We were selling out and the theater, which, like most regional theaters, needed the money, kept pleading with us to extend the run. This meant staying three weeks longer in a city where, in eight weeks, I had not met anyone who had said anything I wanted to put in a play. If anyone from Edmonton is reading this and thinks I am being somewhat harsh on their city, please remember I am talking about the seventies, when the only restaurant that stayed open after a show was a pizza place. Actors customarily eat late at night and, when deprived of their food, tend to get very grouchy. I don't believe room service as we know it today (meaning hot meals) was actually introduced there until the early eighties. Of course, now they have what I believe is the largest shopping mall in the world, with endless miles of fast food to graze upon.

Towards the end of the run, Morton phoned to ask if I'd go into the New York production with Betsy Palmer, currently playing Doris opposite Don Murray, who was about to leave. As a young man, one of my fantasies was to appear in my own play on Broadway, but I was afraid that a few more months of white greasepaint on top of brown hair dye would make me completely bald (at least that's what I told myself), so I passed on the opportunity. Morton tried to change my mind by saying, "But Betsy wants you to do it." This seemed curious, as Betsy had never seen me act, so I asked why. Morton said, "Because you're tall." Not good enough, Morton.

In hindsight, I should have done it. After all, how many chances like that does one get? One reason I refused was that I had a new play about to open, and since the critics now knew I had this terrible thing in my background (situation comedy!), I didn't want to give them any more ammunition. The main reason, though, was that I wouldn't have cast myself as George and felt I was only competent in the role. I am not being falsely modest as I think I am (or was) a very good actor in certain roles … just not in this one. But I still should have done it. As the songwriters Fred Ebb and John Kander wrote, "Say yes!"

The movie rights for *Same Time Next Year* had been sold to Universal, I had written the screenplay, and Walter Mirisch, the producer, had signed Robert Mulligan to direct. Robert is a very good director but made the choice not to see the play, which was still running. This mistake was made by all three directors assigned to film my plays. One actually said he was afraid "it would spoil his vision." Since all three were comedies and over long runs had been polished, with the timing and comic business honed in front of hundreds of audiences, not bothering to see them even to find out where the laughs were seemed truly stupid. In preproduction meetings, when it was suggested that certain lines be cut, I was constantly saying, "Fine, but that's about a thirty-second laugh." If the director had seen the play he would have *known* that.

The usual casting dance took place, with the most unlikely names being bandied about. I don't remember them all but do recall spending a number of hours with Al Pacino and having dozens of suggestions for leading ladies rejected because, in the past, he had had some romantic involvement with them. I finally asked him to give me a list of actresses he had *not* slept with and we could work from that. I kept pushing for Chuck and Ellen, as I felt that the studio would be getting the benefit of all the work they had done on the characters. Unfortunately, it doesn't work that way in Hollywood, where they almost never cast an actor who originally played it on stage. I have the feeling this is because the director likes to believe he is creating an original product and hates to be reminded that the whole film didn't spring full-blown from his brain. I believe this is also why directors don't like writers to be around on the set when the script is being shot, because it reminds everyone that the director is not a creator but an interpreter. The studio wouldn't even consider Chuck, as he wasn't considered a "movie name" (whatever that is), and for a while resisted Ellen, who, even though she had won an Oscar, was deemed to be too old for the film. I believe that her appearance on some television award show, in which she looked particularly fetching, may have been what changed their minds. Shortly after, Alan Alda, who had been one of our top choices for the play, was cast as George.

On the first day of shooting I dropped by the set. I have always had trouble holding a grudge, and it wasn't until I actually saw Ellen again that I vividly remembered how strained our professional involvement had been. Given our past relationship, it might seem odd that I pushed for her to do the film, but it is a fact that it is not necessary to like a person offstage to appreciate that they fulfill the demands of the material on stage. Playwrights, if they're passionate about their work being realized accurately, will always forgive any offstage behavior when the actor in question successfully inhabits the writer's creation. Hence the old punch line, "Remind me never to hire that son of a bitch again ... until I need him!" By the same token, I've had many close friends of mine appear in plays and although we've had a lot of laughs offstage, they haven't satisfied expectations in the theater. Fortunately, I do have many friends who are extraordinarily talented and have often experienced the joy of working with nice people who also give brilliant performances.

Any problems I had working with Ellen again were not really a factor, as I had much less of an emotional involvement in the film than the play and this, plus a busy theater career, kept me away during the shooting. The company went to the Heritage House, near Mendocino, where I had originally conceived the idea, to film but couldn't find a suitable cottage with an ocean vista so, in true movie fashion, they built one themselves. It was more along the lines of a traditional, rustic cabin and I thought not as interesting or attractive as the Spanish-style suite Bill Ritman had designed for the stage. At the end of filming the hotel divided it into two cottages, one bearing the plaque "Same Time" and the other "Next Year." As far as I know they are still there.

When I saw the edited film I was less than enthusiastic. It wasn't a complete embarrassment, but there were a number of factors that made it less effective than the play. Most importantly, the tone had been changed, with the emphasis more on romance than comedy.

This was because the scenes were all played at the same plodding tempo rather than with a variety of pace, as intended in the script. This meant that the comic edge was lost. A great many of today's comedies seem to suffer from this pedantic pacing, and I sometimes think it would be possible to go out and earn a degree in nuclear physics during the pauses between lines. The classic comedies of the thirties and forties, directed by people like Frank Capra, Preston Sturges, or Billy Wilder, all have great pace and with their overlapping dialogue seem to move with the speed of light, constantly taking the audience by surprise. This is the essence of comedy.

Another problem was the casting of Alan Alda. The actors who were the most successful as George had a nervous, kinetic quality, which easily translated into the neurotic behavior important to the character. Alan has constantly shown in the past that he is an excellent actor, but I felt he and George were not a good marriage. Although he has the "tight ass" quality of George, he seems to me to be eminently sane, or at least that's the impression he gives, and I felt his efforts to play the neurosis and paranoia showed. His performance was also hampered by a bad makeup job and at the end of the film, when he was supposed to be fifty-one, he looked close to seventy. I understand that he and Ellen never developed an off-camera rapport and that didn't help, either. Despite these flaws, people who haven't seen the play seem to have enjoyed the movie immensely, and I'm grateful that millions of viewers have had a chance to see the story.

Ellen and I were both nominated for Oscars, the movie more than made its money back, and, some twenty years later, it is still a television staple.

I'll let you in on a secret. Nominated screenwriters almost always know if they are going to win before the actual awards are given out. Nothing crooked here: it's simply that the Writer's Guild Awards precede the Oscars and are a strong indication of how the

Oscars will go. Jill and I didn't attend any of the post-Oscar parties but got into our long, long, white limousine, with a cute girl driver in chauffeur's livery, and headed for a small house in the San Fernando Valley, where we had always watched the award shows with a group of friends. There they consoled me and let me read my "acceptance" speech. And if you want to know what it was, please take a look at the dedication at the beginning of this book.

I have always been a huge fan of musical comedies, believing that they reflect how life *should* be. I even like the bad ones, and as soon as a pit orchestra strikes up my critical faculties desert me. I think one of the reasons I originally wanted to come to North America from England was that, in the late forties, I saw a production of *Annie Get Your Gun*, with Dolores Grey, in the West End and wanted to go where they could do *that*. This is rather ironic because I don't believe the British can produce musicals nearly as well as Americans. Not long ago I went to see *Crazy for You* in London with Simon Callow, the actor, writer, director, restaurant critic, and anything else you can think of. During the intermission he said, "You know the difference between a Broadway chorus line and an English chorus line? The Broadway chorus line is sexy. The British chorus line is just … *jolly*."

Although I'd written dozens of television variety shows while in Canada, I'd never had the chance to work in the field of stage musical comedy until the mid-eighties, when the composer and lyricist Stan Daniels and I got together to write the musical version of *Same Time, Next Year*, retitled *Every Time I See You*. When we failed to get it off the ground in the United States we put it on the shelf until 1994, when the Madach Theater in Budapest wanted to mount a production. They had already produced all of my plays. I had been to Budapest twice and while there had seen some musicals, which had a high standard of production, so we agreed to give them the rights to *Every Time I See You*.

Tamas Szirtes, an old friend of mine who had directed a number of my plays in Hungary, wanted Stan to write an opening number for the show, reasoning that, since the play of *Same Time* had been performed for seven years in Budapest, he wanted to let the audience know right away that this was a musical. This request stumped Stan for a few days as he couldn't think of any characters who could sing it. Then, one night he phoned me with the solution: the bed. The bed? Yes, the bed would "sing" a song called *Everyone Loves Romance* and, during the number, the bed would open up and everyone who had ever slept in it would pop out of it. It worked like a charm.

I didn't attend rehearsals but Stan flew to Budapest to demonstrate the score and then went a second time to see the final days of rehearsal and the previews. Jill and I flew there in time to see the final preview on December 30 and attend the gala opening on New Year's Eve. Stan was very optimistic about the show and predicted that I'd like it. We donned formal wear in the cavernous suite we had been given (I said it felt like the quarters of a Nazi colonel ... turned out it had actually been the wartime suite of a Nazi general) and went to the large theater to join an audience of all the leading lights of the Hungarian performing arts. Filled with pleasant anticipation, we waited for the curtain to go up. But it didn't. Ten minutes went by, then twenty, and then thirty. Finally it rose to reveal the leading man and the director, Tamas Szirtes, standing on the stage. Tamas commenced to speak and, without knowing a word of Hungarian, it was apparent that the leading lady had hurt herself and that there would be no performance that night. In the middle of his speech an elderly lady stood up in the audience and started to cry uncontrollably in loud, racking sobs. We later discovered that she was the actress' mother and that she was an actress herself. Of course. She later told us that, in her day, she had been much more famous than her daughter and was hoping for a comeback. Of course.

We all straggled back to our hotel, got out of our clothes, drank some champagne, and offered up not-so-silent prayers that the pulled ligament in our leading lady's leg would heal enough for her to perform the next night.

It did and she did and we were treated to a sparkling performance capped by twenty-seven curtain calls. Hungarian audiences are very polite and would not think of leaving the theater until all the calls are taken. That night, these included sustained applause for Stan and me, who were summoned up on the stage to join the cast, presented with huge bouquets of flowers, and hugged by the leading players. Not a bad way to see in the New Year. The show ran for two years.

Although I would go on to write many more plays, none so far have achieved the popularity of *Same Time, Next Year*, which has been translated into over thirty foreign languages, been given thousands of performances in prestigious theaters like the Old Vic in London and the Anton Chekhov in Moscow, and constantly enjoyed revivals. Sometimes many years will go by between the times that I am reluctantly pushed into watching a production. When I do, it's as if I'm visiting an old girlfriend for whom I still have great affection but no longer feel passionate about. Jill prefers to compare it to a dutiful older child who keeps sending money home. Anyway, I feel distanced from the play ... almost as if I didn't write it.

In fact, many people think I *didn't* write it. The following is an excerpt from a letter I recently received from Neil Simon:

> I am almost a guilty but flattered recipient of compliments when people tell me how much they enjoyed my *Same Time, Next Year*. The best one was from Shelly Winters, whom I met at a theater one night.

SHELLY "I think *Same Time, Next Year* is one of your best plays."
ME "I didn't write it."
SHELLY "Why not?"

About two years ago someone told me that there was an answer on the TV show *Jeopardy* of *Same Time, Next Year*. The question: "What is the most-produced two-character play in history?" This prompted me to sit down and write a sequel, called *Same Time, Another Year*.

But that's another story.

★ Tribute to a funny man

After the production of *Same Time* my mind kept playing with the idea of writing Jerry Davis as a character. Over a period of weeks I developed an idea about a father who never manages to have a relationship with his twenty-year-old son, an industrious, responsible boy with little use for frivolity, who is the exact opposite of his charming, apparently superficial father. My idea, in simplistic terms, was that the boy represented the adult in us while the father embodied the child. To heighten the conflict, I put a "clock" on the play by having the father threatened by a fatal illness.

The structure of the play came about after I had attended a memorial for Harold Clurman at the Schubert Theater in New York and decided to use a tribute in a theater as a framework for the evening.

Tribute was rewritten more than any of my other plays. I wasn't interested in using the events of Jerry's life but rather the essence of his character, which helped the leading role of Scottie Templeton immediately come off the page. The problem was that the character was so charismatic it made creating a formidable adversary in the role of the son extremely difficult. There was another unforeseen hurdle. As someone instilled with the ideals of moral responsibility and discipline, I assumed my sympathies would favor the boy's point of view, but instead, as the writing of the play progressed, I found, much to my surprise, that I was clearly empathizing with the careless wastrel of the father. Characters who make us laugh are usually sympathetic so I knew it wouldn't be easy to sway the affection in the direction of the son. But I persisted and, after about eight versions of the son, finally thought I had a draft ready to be seen.

The first person I gave it to was Jerry. I wasn't sure what his reaction would be, but it wasn't anything I could possibly have imagined. It wasn't that he was critical—far from it, he praised the play highly as a marvelous piece of work. But there was something wrong, something I couldn't quite put my finger on. Finally, after a number of days, I told him that our friendship meant more to me than the play and, although it in no way mirrored the events of his life, if it bothered him, I would burn it. He protested that he couldn't let me do this—it was too good a play. Thinking that perhaps he thought I was making money using his personality I told him that I planned to give him a third of my proceeds from the play. He was extremely grateful for this, but I sensed there was still something amiss, and the slight strain between us persisted until one day I confronted him and said, "Look, Jerry, you're not looking me in the eye. We're too good of friends for this to go on. You have to tell me what's bothering you."

He looked at me and said, "I should have written this play. And my problem is that I know I never would have."

Fortunately, our friendship not only stayed intact but flourished until the day he died at the age of seventy-four in 1991. I was with him at the hospital after he had a stroke and was about to go in for the operation he wouldn't survive. Aware that his friends thought of him as Peter Pan, he said, "Wires are beginning to show, huh, kid?" I still miss him.

The ironic part to all this is that most people in show business believe the character of Scottie was based not on Jerry, but on his boyhood friend, Harvey Orkin. Harvey was an agent with a colorful personality, whom I had only met very briefly once, so at first I was puzzled about the misunderstanding. I later put the pieces together and now believe it happened due to a combination of events. Like Scottie in the play, Harvey Orkin had recently suffered a fatal illness. Added to this was that Jerry, who had been amused by him all his life, had absorbed many of his mannerisms and speech patterns. The misunderstanding was cemented when Jack Lemmon, who also knew Harvey, told a newspaper interviewer that the character he was playing was based on him.

Harvey's widow, Gisella, saw one of the previews in New York and told me that she was pleased at how well I'd captured her husband. What was I to say? I said, "I'm glad you liked it."

When I sent the play to Morton Gottlieb, who had been expecting an out-and-out comedy, he reacted with some consternation. He phoned me and, without even a "hello," said, "It's about a man dying!" I said that it wasn't about a man dying but a man living. He said, "That's what all playwrights say who write plays about a man dying."

Believing it wasn't commercial enough for Broadway, he suggested sending the play to Arthur Storch, who was then head of the drama department of Syracuse University, to see if he'd be interested in trying it out there without any big-name actors. I agreed and that's how Arthur Storch came to direct the play.

I never write roles for specific actors for a number of reasons. First of all, I am always afraid that I'll end up with the personality of the *actor* on the page rather than an original character, and secondly, I know that if the actor isn't available I will have a difficult time finding someone who can play it. However, after I'd completed the first draft, the only performer I believed to be perfect was Jack Lemmon. Morton thought there was no chance he would be able to get him to return to Broadway, as he hadn't been on the

New York stage for many years. But knowing that all I had to lose was a script, I mailed him a copy, along with a note saying that I couldn't think of anyone who could play Scottie better than he and I'd be a fool not to at least offer it to him. I really didn't hold out much hope of his accepting the role and more or less forgot about it until just before we were due to leave for the *Same Time* rehearsals in Edmonton, when I received a call from an associate of Jack. He told me that he was "going to lock Jack in a room and not let him out until he'd read it." A day after we arrived in Edmonton Jack phoned me himself to say that somehow he had to do the play but since he had commitments lined up it would be almost a year before he'd be free. Would we be willing to wait? We were.

When I phoned Morton to tell him the news he immediately abandoned all thoughts of a production in Syracuse. We were going to Broadway.

★ Jack Lemmon and the man who was a poached egg ★

★ The plan was to open *Tribute* at the by now familiar Colonial Theater in Boston, play a month there, move to the Royal Alexandra in Toronto for another month, and then to the Brooks Atkinson Theater for its New York run. *Same Time*, still playing at the Atkinson, would be moved to another theater, but we had the use of the theater to conduct auditions for the other roles in *Tribute*.

I have always loathed auditions, both as an actor hoping to be chosen for a part, and as a writer in a position to have some input into the hiring of the auditioners. Although I was a fairly good "sight reader," I can't remember ever getting a part through an audition. I do remember some very embarrassing moments, though. Once, desperately needing work, I was called to read for a role in an industrial show that called for both singing and acting. Now, I do not sing—I have a good musical ear, but, perhaps because of that, I do not sing. My plan was to so dazzle them with my acting ability that my bad singing would be deemed unimportant. The auditions were held in the nontheatrical venue of a room in a large Toronto office building. When I arrived I was dismayed to see that all my fellow auditioners not only had briefcases stuffed with music but that some of them even had their own accompanists.

My request that I read first was denied and when I told them I had no song prepared they gave me fifteen minutes to come up with something. I retreated to a large, empty men's washroom, planted myself in front of a mirror, locked eyes with my reflection, and launched into a tender, overly emotional rendition of *It Had To Be You*. Midway through the second chorus I sensed another presence—that odd feeling when you just *know* someone else is in the room. I shifted my gaze to see the reflection of two men, conservatively clad, standing just inside the door, faces immobile, eyes mirroring disbelief. They noticed I had seen them and, without saying a word, quickly exited. I never went back to the audition.

Another experience had a happier ending. During my days as a summer-stock actor I had always played either leading or very large roles. This was not due to any blinding talent but more because of an aptitude for being able to blend greasepaint and use crepe hair in a way that made me look old enough for juicy character parts. This created in me a totally unwarranted arrogance when looking for work on TV and a complete disdain for any of the five-line parts I was occasionally offered. To be frank, I still don't agree with the old adage, "There are no small parts, only small actors." Most small parts are boring and unrewarding, which is why, when I do write a small part, I try to at least give the actor a "moment" that will let him or her shine. Anyway, one day when Jill was pregnant and out of commission as an actress and we badly needed money, she answered a phone call from a producer of children's programs for the Canadian Broadcasting Corporation, who asked her if I'd be available to play a crow. She guessed what my reaction would be, so when I got home she casually mentioned that I should phone the CBC. When I asked her why, she said she didn't know. As I dialed she quickly retreated to the kitchen, where she listened to the following conversation.

Me This is Bernard Slade. Would I play a what?——I don't play animals or birds, I play people——How much money?——I see. Well, maybe I could——You mean now? (*A pause*) Caw, caw, caw!

I got the part and it paid the rent that month.

Watching actors audition is uncomfortable because, apart from empathizing with their tension, it is usually the first time I hear any of the play read out loud. This can be profoundly discouraging if the material is read badly and can make me believe the entire project is doomed. I once hired an actress as an understudy because, even though she was far too young for the part, she read it so well it restored my faith in the play.

The casting of *Tribute* proceeded smoothly and we quickly cast A. Larry Haines, Teresa Hughes, Joan Wells, Catharine Hicks, and Rosemary Prinz. The key part of the son went to a young actor named Robert Picardo. Feeling fortunate that we had managed to put together such a talented cast, I returned to California to await the start of rehearsals.

During the play the character of Scottie sits at the piano and plays an original composition. Jack Lemmon is an excellent pianist and he told me he had written a piece of music that might work, so I invited him to the house to play it. When he arrived he looked nervous, and when I finally got him to the piano he went into an involved disclaimer about the tune that was longer than a Theodore Bikel introduction to an obscure Rumanian folk song. The song was marvelous. Everything augured well. Then I got a phone call from the director Arthur Storch.

Arthur said he had some disturbing news: he had received a call from Bob Picardo, the young actor we had hired to play Jud, the son, who had told him that all his hair was falling out. Bob was concerned that when we saw him again we might not recognize him. I was having trouble grasping this. "You mean that juvenile with a full head of hair we hired three weeks ago is going to walk into rehearsals totally bald?" Arthur said, "Apparently." When I suggested the use of a toupee, Arthur went into a long dissertation about how it wasn't just the hair loss that worried him but that it might be a manifestation of some deep psychological disturbance.

When I got off the phone I called my agent, Jack Hutto, who was, and still is, quite bald and asked him how quickly he had lost his hair. "Oh, practically overnight," he said. "Came out in clumps." This didn't reassure me. Before we went into rehearsal the rest of the cast were given the puzzling instruction that when acting with Bob they "were never to touch his hair."

Bob went on to have a very successful career starring in the TV series *China Beach* (with toupee) and one of the *Star Trek* series (without), and we are still good friends. He eventually told me his end of the story of how, panic stricken, he had tried various toupees, hair weaves, etc., in a desperate attempt to look like the same young man we'd hired. Once, when walking together in New York, we saw a drunk lying in the gutter. Bob said, "Did you ever notice how deadbeat drunks always have a full head of hair? He doesn't even need it. I'm a twenty-five-year-old actor who does need it and I'm bald!"

This reminds me of an actor friend of mine, whom we'll call George (because that's his name), who is known for his "method" approach to his craft, and his intensity and the amount of energy he invests into any role he portrays. After successfully auditioning for a part, the director casually indicated my friend's thinning hair and said, "Of course, we'll get you a toupee to give you a full head of hair." George fixed him with a stare and said, "I can *play* hair!"

Our rehearsals were held in one of the upstairs rooms of the Minskov Theater, and the bright space with the magnificent views of New York seemed to complement the aura of good cheer surrounding the cast. This was to be just about the happiest company ever brought together for any of my plays. This was largely due to Jack, who effortlessly created a stress-free mood by behaving like a fellow actor rather than a "star." It was indicative that, once we moved into a theater, any informal gatherings or note-giving sessions always took place in his dressing room. The company was on the road together for two months before opening in New York, and this also contributed to the closeness of the actors, who in many cases still maintain ongoing friendships. I believe another factor motivating the unusual harmony was that the constellation of the company mirrored a real family, with Jack as the father, Larry as the genial uncle, Teresa as the eccentric aunt, Joan as the sexy cousin, and Bob and Cathy as the kids. There is a theory that actors move through a succession of theatrical families, always looking to replace their own real families. If this is the case, ours certainly fulfilled all the requirements.

I had been hearing Jack's voice in my head all during the rewriting and at the first reading he was just as brilliant as I had imagined. His unerring instinct about the part continued throughout the rehearsals until the first run-through, when he unaccountably fell into all the traps of self-pity inherent in the role and was just awful. After the run-through, with the director also present, I spoke to him for about forty minutes, enumerating all the things I felt were wrong with his performance. During my monologue he didn't say a word, and at the end of my harangue there was a long pause. Trying to lighten the moment, I said, "Look, I feel ridiculous telling one of the best actors in the world how to act." He said, "No, that's okay. Do you have notes?" I gave him my written notes, but he didn't mention them until the following night, when four of us were having dinner and he suddenly turned to me and said, "Look, I read your notes. I agree with most of them, but there was one thing you said that really offended me. It upset me so much I almost phoned you at four this morning." I thought, "Okay, here it comes—good-bye, Mr. Nice Guy." I asked what had bothered him so much. He said, "What did you mean, *one* of the best actors in the world?" Nice to work with someone with a sense of humor.

When we moved to the Colonial Theater in Boston and I got a first look at the set I was disappointed. I felt that I was partly responsible because with all my other plays I had been very specific about the set I wanted, but, for some reason, I felt I had been restricting Bill Ritman's creativity, and so with *Tribute* I had only given him a general idea. The set he devised didn't really help the play, and he wasn't happy with his work, either, but we were stuck with it.

The second surprise came at the dress rehearsal, when it was discovered that the costume designer had outfitted everyone in various shades of beige. Since the set was also beige it looked like the cast was about to break into a song akin to the Ascot musical number from *My Fair Lady*. Luckily, Jack was traveling with dozens of suitcases filled with his own clothes, which we put to good use, and by substituting off-the-rack dresses for the women, we were able to dispense with the monochromatic look on the stage. All the costume problems seemed to be solved until Jack enthusiastically presented us with an idea. His notion was that, since the character would be going through chemotherapy, he wanted to wear clothes three sizes too big for him to emphasize the weight loss. I was totally against the idea, believing that we should downplay the illness of the character, but before I could voice my objections, Jill quietly said, "Scottie's a very vain man, Jack. Don't you think he'd have his suits altered to fit?" Jack saw the logic in this and agreed. Whew!

Tribute opened to highly appreciative audiences and good critical response and, once again, I was left with very little actual rewriting to do. The only hiccup occurred early in the run, when during Jack's final, emotional soliloquy we heard odd clicking noises all over the auditorium, coupled with the most dreaded sound in the theater—coughing. This puzzled us as we all felt this section was one of the most effective in the play. The next night, during Jack's monologue, I sat in a box where I could see the audience, and the reason for the sounds became immediately apparent. The clicking noises were being caused by women opening their purses to extract Kleenex tissues, while the coughing was the result of men clearing their emotionally restricted throats.

There is a line in which Scottie Templeton says, "When a friend dies you lose a friend. When *you* die you lose all your friends." I didn't intend this to be funny. The audience screamed with laughter. I asked Jack if he could kill this laugh. He looked at me as if I was crazy and I felt like I was trying to take a new toy from a happy three-year-old. When I explained that I believed it came at the wrong time in the scene and was a "bad laugh," he considered the suggestion and that night, always the playwright's friend, artfully squelched the laugh.

Jerry Davis flew in to see the play and, a few lines after the opening curtain, started to audibly sob. Other members of the audience turned to look at him, all quite bewildered by, as Jerry put it, "This broken, old Jew sobbing his eyes out while the rest of the audience were falling about laughing." I stayed away from him at intermission and when I approached him after the final curtain he excused himself to "make some repairs" in the washroom. I noticed that he had gone into the women's washroom by mistake. But he didn't come out. Not for twenty minutes. When he did reappear he was with three "new friends" he'd met in the ladies' lounge, who were fascinated by the fact that he was "the real Scottie Templeton." It turned out that he loved the production, although he felt that "Jack wasn't as charming as he was."

There was another character in the play who was based on a real-life counterpart. Doctor Elsie Giorgi was one of the most remarkable women I have ever known and I used her persona to create the character of Doctor Petrelli in the play. A disheveled woman of indeterminate age, with a casual manner and a strong

New York accent, Elsie had not entered medical school until she was twenty-eight, at a time when female doctors were a rarity. She spent the rest of her life devoted to medicine and her patients ranged from destitute, homeless people to internationally known movie stars. I met her shortly after I arrived in LA and my wife, knowing my aversion to members of the medical profession, convinced me to see Elsie for a checkup by saying, "She's not like other doctors." She wasn't. Even her offices were different: comfortable armchairs covered in chintz and walls boasting the artwork of her younger patients along with such homilies as, "It's not what you eat, it's what's eating you." A visit to Elsie, who always insisted that you "eat a little something" before you talked, was more like a visit to a favorite aunt than a physician. During my first visit, while she was giving me an internal rectal examination, she said, "Am I hurting you or are you tense?" I said, "I'm tense." She said, "Are you tense because I'm a woman?" I said, "No, I get tense when *anybody* does that to me." This cracked her up and, over the years, I was the recipient of a lot of chicken soup and heard the most outrageous medical stories in the world.

When *Tribute* played in Los Angeles Elsie went backstage after the show to meet Theresa Hughes, who was playing the fictionalized Doctor Petrelli. She said, "Now listen, dearie," (she called everyone "dearie") "You've almost got me down perfectly, but there are a couple of things I can help you with, so come into my office tomorrow and we'll have lunch." And they did.

Comedy writers are literary magpies: if something strikes their funny bone they will purloin it and stash it away until they can find a place to use it. My sister Shirley and her husband John owned a four-hundred-year-old pub for many years called The Bell Inn in the small English village of Outwood. One day I was expounding on my theory that the British had more eccentrics, and tolerated them better, than Americans. My sister said, "Oh, I don't know," and turned to her husband. "We don't have that many eccentrics come into the pub, do we?" He said, "Not really. Of course, there's old Tom, who thinks he's a poached egg." I said, "He thinks he's a poached egg?" John said, "Oh, not all the time, just a few times a month." Fascinated, I asked, "How can you tell when these times are?" John said, "He carries a small brown mat around with him. That's his toast. He sits in the middle of it and nobody is allowed to step on his toast." Of course, I mentally filed this away and some years later included it in *Tribute*. When Shirley and John flew to New York to see the play I met them after the performance in a restaurant. They are my biggest fans, and after excessively complimenting me about the play, Shirley said, "You know what's odd? *We* know someone who thinks he's a poached egg." I said, "Shirley, where do you think I got it? You think there are *two* people we know who think they are poached eggs?"

As the run progressed it became apparent that the audience, most of whom had been imprinted over the years by a string of wonderful performances by Jack in extremely sympathetic "everyman" film roles, were not willing to recognize the dark side of Scottie's character. This made it difficult for Bob Picardo, playing Jud, to engender the sympathy the character deserved. After the first performance, Bob jokingly said, "Not only did the audience hate me, but at the intermission the rest of the *cast* stopped speaking to me!" There wasn't much I could do about this, as I couldn't very well tell Jack to be less funny and charming. Part of this imbalance was due to the fact that the majority of the audience was the same age as the character of Scottie and could more readily identify with his problems than with those of the son. This flaw was never entirely solved, although later, when we played to younger audiences, I felt that the understanding of the two leading characters was more evenly balanced.

We continued to play to SRO audiences, with the cast, especially Jack, giving what I later realized were the best performances they would ever deliver. There is a theory that plays shouldn't stay out of town too long in a pre-Broadway run because performances will lose their edge. I have found this to be true and believe the performances in all my plays were best in the early days of the run. I think the adrenaline produced by the tension of being unfamiliar with a piece generated a certain electricity. Fortunately, when we moved to the beautiful Royal Alexandra in my old hometown of Toronto we were still in good shape.

Canadian expatriates who have left to pursue careers elsewhere have found that the Canadian press has always been tougher on their work than newspaper critics in other countries, so I was not surprised when the reviews ranged from ecstatic raves to fairly vicious attacks. These in no way affected the box office and we were totally sold out for the run.

The engagement in Toronto was very pleasant, with reunions with old friends and parties given for and by the cast, who seemed to have managed not to dwell on the Broadway opening facing us after our run at the Royal Alex was finished.

One of the parties was given for us by an old, dear friend, Barbara Hamilton, who was a well-known Canadian actress. On the way to the party I shared a taxi with Jack and Felicia Lemmon, and mentioned that Barbara lived with a man named Wayne Lonergan, who had served twenty-five years in jail for the murder of his wife. Jack got very excited and began to talk about how he remembered the case as one of the most notorious of the twentieth century. I interrupted him by saying, "Look, we never talk about this in front of Barbara or Wayne so please don't mention it, Jack." He said that he wouldn't, but, just to make sure, I reiterated, "Look, you have to promise that you won't bring it up." He said that of course he wouldn't. About half an hour after we arrived Barbara, who still drank in those days and was somewhat tipsy, approached Jack and said in a slurred voice, "You know what your performance does to people? See that man over there that I live with? He's a convicted killer and you made him cry like a baby!" Jack turned his head to look at me with a "take" impossible to describe.

A string of pearls and two broken legs

Tribute opened in New York on May 31, 1979, at the Brooks Atkinson Theater, which *Same Time* had vacated by moving a few blocks north to the Ambassador Theater, so I was able to enjoy the heady sensation of having two plays on Broadway at the same time. I didn't see the opening night performance. Jill watched the show sitting beside Felicia Lemmon on some stairs at the back of the theater, both extremely nervous, and both clutching the strings of pearls they were wearing. At precisely the same moment, their strings broke and the pearls slowly rolled down the aisle towards the stage. I don't know about Felicia's, but Jill's were fake. Jill told me that it was not one of Jack's best performances. Warren Crane, our stage manager, told me it was probably his worst. This is fairly common with opening night performances and, if we must have critics, it is perhaps a good argument in favor of staggering their attendance over three performances, which they do today.

The party after the show was held at the Tavern on the Green restaurant. Jack's celebrity had attracted dozens of fellow celebrities, and they in turn attracted the press, whom Morton had elected to admit. It may have been good for publicity, but it made for a lousy party, with tables reserved for the cast and production staff being taken over by noisy reporters swilling down free booze and food. The reason Morton wanted the press there became apparent about half an hour into the party, when he announced that, because we had done such good business on the road, all the investors would be getting their money back that night. He asked them all to form a line in front of him and doled out the checks. It made all the papers, since this had never been done before.

Jill and I managed to locate a table away from the raucous festivities and were flabbergasted to see John Simon join us. I had never heard of a major critic attending the opening night party of a play he had just reviewed, much less talking to the playwright. I have always avoided meeting critics, afraid that I would be excessively hostile or nauseatingly charming, but when Simon joined us the encounter went pleasantly enough. Perhaps this was because I assumed that, since he'd come to the party, his review would be favorable. Morton is much less delicate in his dealings with critics, and after the opening of *Same Time*, when we were putting together a full page ad of quotes, my naïveté was dented as I overheard him on the phone with Rex Reed, saying, "Look, we don't have a quote from you. Do you want to be in the ad or not?" Of course he did. They have careers to further, too. The enthusiastic review of Clive Barnes, now writing for the *New York Post*, came in and was read aloud, sending the already loud gathering up another decibel level. Emotionally exhausted, my brain throbbing from trying to speak in perfect syntax to John Simon, who also wrote a language column, I escaped to the washroom.

When I emerged ten minutes later the first thing I sensed was how *quiet* the room had become. One look around and I knew why. Except for a few clusters of people, the room was empty. I moved over to our press agent, Millie Schoenbraun, and asked where Morton was. She told me he had gone home. "What about the *Times* review?" I asked. She grimaced, "We got the *Times* review. Not good."

Jack had not been told about this, so I was faced with breaking the bad news. He looked at me for a moment and then said, "Well, it seems that we're not going to go through this entirely unscathed." Jack's behavior through both success and failure is perhaps the quality I most admire in him, and I wish every writer could have the pleasure of his company.

The *Times* review was written by Richard Eder, who spent only a short time wreaking damage on the New York theatrical world. I've always thought that the reason his notice didn't harm us too much was that his reviews were always written in such a boring manner not even avid theatergoers could finish them. He later took to writing equally tedious book reviews for the *Los Angeles Times*, which were of great service to local insomniacs.

Anyway, the play, bolstered by a glowing three-page review by John Simon in *New York* magazine and by Jack's drawing power, continued to run, quickly building to capacity houses over a six-month run when the show, with two cast changes, moved to the Huntington Hartford Theater in Los Angeles. We had hoped to replace Jack with a star of equal stature but were unsuccessful, and I was treated to the novel experience of having a play close both in New York and LA while it was playing to sold-out houses.

Tribute was subsequently produced all over the world, but I have never seen any actor other than Jack play Scottie Templeton. The national company starred Van Johnson, who broke his ankle the day of the opening in St. Louis. When an urgent call was put in to Jack, who at the time was fishing with his son in Alaska, to see if he could fly in and go on for Van, it was learned that Jack, too, had broken his leg. Make of that what you will, but since then I've never told an actor to "break a leg." Van went on in a wheelchair.

The film of *Tribute* was put together as a coproduction deal between a Hollywood studio and the Canadian producer Garth Drabinsky. To obtain some Canadian government financing a certain percentage of the cast had to be Canadian, but in some cases (with Colleen Dewhurst, for example) I got the feeling they were stretching the requirements and casting people who were only *conceived* in Canada. I again wrote the script and again the director had never seen the play. Maybe this is what made him fall into the trap of making the film overly sentimental, without the saving grace of comedy. I believe that, with the possible exception of Lee Remick, who, as the ex-wife, gave her usual stylish performance, every member of the Broadway cast was superior to the actors in the film.

Fortunately, I was protected from seeing all the mistakes made during the shooting (there was not a thing I could have done about them) by the fact that, following a by now familiar pattern, I was heavily involved with my next Broadway play, *Romantic Comedy*.

Romantic Comedy: a valentine

The first draft of *Romantic Comedy* had been written while I was waiting for Jack Lemmon to be free for rehearsals of *Tribute*, and a rereading of the script after the opening had convinced me that it needed some work. I was put on the right track when my daughter, Laurie, told Jill, "You know, I think Dad feels he's based the character of the playwright on himself. He's written this sarcastic, arrogant, rather cold man, and the pathetic thing is he thinks it's *charming*!" I have always found it odd how many people assume that male playwrights base the men in their plays upon themselves, while quite forgetting that they also create the women. Actually, I've always felt that I was more like the female character Phoebe than Jason, but perhaps that's wishful thinking. Anyway, I immediately wrote a new scene that showed Jason being more warm and vulnerable.

The genesis of *Romantic Comedy* came from three unrelated notions. Some twenty years before, I had read an interview with Ernest Hemingway in which he described himself and Marlene Dietrich as being "the victims of unsynchronized passion," and the phrase had stuck in my mind. I also had been fascinated by the emotional ramifications of writing partnerships, which I felt in many ways mirrored a marriage. The third stimulus was a desire to write a valentine to all the romantic comedies that had influenced me when I was young. I underscored the last notion by designing the piece to be played in three acts rather than the usual two, in a set that would evoke memories of all the plays that had so enchanted audiences in the thirties and forties. Since the play took place over a period of years, I devised some contemporary barriers to the consummation of the protagonists' romance.

I suppose every playwright has a favorite scene in each play that he or she has written and I am no exception, but before I even begin to actually start writing, I need to imagine a scene that will so excite me it forces me to sit down and put pen to paper. In the case of *Romantic Comedy* it was the fight scene at the end of Act Two. I almost always write my plays in sequence, starting with Scene One, but I broke this pattern when I wrote this scene in the play first.

The previous action is that a temperamental leading lady has been giving Phoebe and Jason trouble by badgering them to change the text. When Phoebe and the agent, Blanche, arrive home early one day they discover, much to their surprise, Jason and the actress together, who claim to have been having a "script conference." However, they gradually become aware that the actress is wearing her dress inside out, with the labels prominently exposed. The actress and the agent exit and the scene continues from there.

PHOEBE (*In a dry, strained voice*) You went to bed with her, didn't you?
JASON You want me to stand up and share it with the rest of the class?
PHOEBE Don't deny it.
JASON Look, do you want to fix this play or not?
PHOEBE (*Stares at him, absolutely stunned, her worst fears confirme*d) My God, how could you!
JASON Well—it wasn't easy. (*She is staring at him, her eyes, welling up with tears*) Phoebe, I didn't commit an axe murder! Why are you staring at me like that?

PHOEBE It—it's—so unprofessional!

JASON Actually, it was *very* professional.

PHOEBE (*Tightly, turning away*) Well, I'm glad she has some technique *somewhere.*

JASON What I mean was it *started* out as a professional thing. (*A trifle desperately*) Look, I did it for you too.

PHOEBE (*Icily*) Did I enjoy it?

JASON I was just trying to … improve my relationship with her. What are you doing?

PHOEBE Packing.

JASON Wait a minute—there has to be more to this than an artistic difference of opinion. Just what is bothering you?

PHOEBE (*Stops packing, looks at him*) Bothering me? All right, I'll tell you what's bothering me. I don't like you anymore! You're a vain, arrogant, insensitive, selfish bully!

JASON I am not vain.

PHOEBE (*Stabs a finger in the direction of the sofa*) Then why do you always sit on that couch? (*Jason is nonplussed*) So you can look at yourself all day in (*pointing at mirror*) *that* mirror. I think you're about to get an idea, but you're *admiring* yourself.

JASON (*Coldly*) Is that all?

PHOEBE No, it's not. Whenever we eat in a restaurant you always take the best seat with your back to the wall so everyone can see you.

JASON And so they can't see you! You dress like a walking garage sale!

PHOEBE (*She moves to bookshelf to get a book*) My father has a word for people like you—"jerk"!

JASON I see your gift for language runs in the family.

PHOEBE You said you liked my father.

JASON I lied. Your father is a boring, illiterate old poop! (*Pointing at the book she is holding*) Wait a minute—that book was given to both of us!

PHOEBE It was given to me!

JASON Read the inscription!

PHOEBE Oh, keep the damned book! (*She throws it at him and it hits him in the chest*)

JASON You could have broken a rib! I mean, who do you think you are?

PHOEBE (*Hysterically*) I'll tell you who I am! You're full of shit—that's who I am! (*He is too astounded to reply. She goes back to packing*) God, I'll be so glad not to have to face you every day!

JASON (*Angered*) You think it's been easy living with your relentless perkiness all these years? Have you any idea how depressing it is to be around that much—niceness?

PHOEBE (*Thrown*) Niceness is depressing?

JASON Mealymouthed niceness! Like that time when that actress propositioned you. She asked, "Are you gay?" and do you know what you said?

PHOEBE (*Puzzled*) I said, "No, I'm not."

JASON No, you didn't. You said, "No, I'm not—*but thank you for asking*"! (*He moves to desk*) Here, you want to take some paper? (*Throwing objects from desk*) Paper clips? Used typewriter ribbons? Wait a minute—there's a half-box of Kleenex in the dressing room!

PHOEBE I'm walking out of here with exactly what I came in with!

JASON Plus fifty percent of my royalties!

PHOEBE Which I more than earned!

JASON And from which you have the first nickel—plus towels and soap from every hotel we ever stayed in. You know what I really despise about you? I loathe your——

PHOEBE Cheapness.

JASON You're finishing my sentences for me!

PHOEBE *Someone* has to do it!

JASON (*Infuriated*) You really want to know what I've always hated about you?

PHOEBE Why not? You've gone this far.

JASON I've always hated your ass!

PHOEBE Eloquent. Very eloquent.

JASON I mean *literally hate your ass*! You and your damned exercises. Every morning for ten years I turn around and find I'm addressing your rear end. Believe me, it's not a pretty sight!

PHOEBE (*Hurt, fighting back tears*) Yes—well—I think I'll get a second opinion on that. Good-bye, Jason.

JASON Phoebe, you can't leave. (*A last desperate plea*) I named one of my children after you!

PHOEBE (*Finally, quietly*) It's not enough, Jason. (*She goes to close the suitcase, but it is so loaded it won't close. In a mixture of frustration and rage, she kicks the case*) Oh, to hell with it! (*She takes a small tank of goldfish under her arm and crosses to the door*)

JASON It won't last, you know. Once he sees those substandard flannel nightgowns he'll run for the nearest fire escape! (*This really stings her. She turns around*)

PHOEBE (*With dignity*) I have only one reply to that. Even an egg takes three minutes!

JASON (*Baffled*) What?

PHOEBE (*Tearfully yelling*) You were inadequate in Chicago! (*She slams the door, leaving an outraged Jason. He crosses to the overstuffed suitcase and violently kicks it. It flies open and the impact jolts the tape recorder inside, and the music "But Not for Me" fills the room. The anger drains out of him as he lifts the recorder out of the debris. He puts the recorder down, notices her red baseball cap on top of all the junk. He picks it up, crosses slowly to the sofa, sits dejectedly, puts cap on head*)

JASON Oh, Phoebe—you always were such a sloppy sentimentalist. *The curtain slowly falls.*

The scene always worked like a charm, and when student actors tell me that they are working on a scene from *Romantic Comedy* in class it invariably turns out to be this section of the play.

For anyone interested in the craft of comedy writing perhaps it is worth pointing out that, although the scene gets big laughs, very few of the lines are funny if taken out of context. The laughs are realized because of character, relationship, and situation. The term "one-liners" is often used by people who don't actually know what that phrase means. "Take my wife ... please!" is a one-liner used for years by the comic Henny Youngman, but very few playwrights employ that form of comedy. One of the funniest exchanges in modern comedy is in *Born Yesterday*. Billie Dawn says, "Do me a favor, will you, Harry?" He says, "What's that?" She says, "Drop dead." Hardly side splitting on its own, and only funny when said after her relationship with Harry Brock has been established and the situation in the play fully developed.

This aspect of writing is not easily learned, and I am grateful for the years of appearing in so many of the best modern stage comedies, which made me appreciate the importance of the fundamentals of working in this exacting medium.

★ Mia Farrow, Tony Perkins, and balls in the air ★

Upon reflection, the desire to write a valentine to all the romantic comedies I had seen and appeared in was largely because the attractive drawing rooms, peopled with charming men and women, represented a life that was never part of my background. Given my nomadic youth, lived out in impoverished flats and suburban lower-middle-class houses, it is easy to understand why the glamour and feeling of permanence displayed in these plays would appeal to my romantic sensibilities. Of course, I was aware that they didn't reflect "real life," but there is no question that all those paneled rooms with French doors and cozy fireplaces were part of the reason I got into the theater. I was not alone in my attraction: after the play was produced I heard from many performers of my generation who also became actors because of the rose-colored vision presented in this genre of plays.

Morton liked the play and the production started to come together quickly, with Joe Hardy signed to direct and Michael Caine expressing an interest in playing Jason. We had sent the script to Michael but, because he hadn't worked in the theater for many years, didn't expect he would be willing to commit to a run. I met him for lunch in LA and learned that not only did he want to do it but that he liked the script so much he wanted to invest in the production. We approached Blythe Danner about playing

Phoebe and she was also enthusiastic about the play. We seemed to be on our way. But then our progress was stalled by a peculiar "good news, bad news" situation.

The script had not been formally submitted to any film studio, but somehow it fell into the hands of Universal Studios (they have their ways), who were interested in buying the film rights. I am sure that this was partly because *Same Time, Next Year* had already been filmed but not yet released and, believing they were going to have a massive hit, they wanted to follow it with another script of mine. My business manager, Murray Neidorf, made what is known in Hollywood as a "very rich deal" for the property. As an aside, this was for an astounding amount of money that even today has rarely been equaled. The only caveat was that the studio did not want to be locked into using Michael Caine in the film who, at that point, was going through a trough in his movie career. Michael, believing that to do the play and not the movie would be committing "professional suicide," decided against doing it on Broadway. Blythe Danner subsequently withdrew because she felt that Phoebe was too much like the character she had played in *Butterflies Are Free*. This was quite baffling as the two characters were as much alike as Lady Macbeth and Billie Dawn. However, there are many ways of saying "no," and we were left with no leading actors.

The usual casting dance started and, as usual, we were treated to the standard number of rejections. What made the problem more acute was that the movie contract was predicated upon there being a Broadway production of the play, and I was beginning to fear that with no stars in the offing there might not be a stage version and we would lose the millions of dollars involved in the film deal.

I am not sure where the notion of Mia Farrow playing Phoebe originated, but I assume it came from someone in Morton's office.

It certainly wasn't my idea, and when I heard it I was totally against the suggestion because even though I was aware of her having done one or two plays in England, I associated her with film and TV work. I voiced my objection to Morton with, "What are we going to do—put a mike around her neck?" Morton said, "Bern, she absolutely adores your play." I immediately capitulated, mumbling, "Well, maybe she'll be okay." This about-face was not entirely due to vanity, as I'd learned that if an actor is passionate about playing a role the chances are good that they will be successful. It turned out that not only did we not have to amplify her voice but that Mia had the best theater voice I'd ever heard, speaking with an unforced clarity that effortlessly reached the back row of the theater. Playwrights, of course, love this ability, and in the play there is an exchange in which Phoebe asks about an actress, "Do you love her, Jason?" and he replies, "Love her? I can't even hear her from the balcony!"

With Mia already committed, it was easier to attract a leading man, and shortly afterwards Tony Perkins was cast as Jason. Undeterred by the fact that we were about to present a romantic comedy featuring the stars of *Psycho* and *Rosemary's Baby*, we launched into auditions on both coasts for the other roles. Carole Cook, an old friend of mine and wife of Tom Troupe, who had played in the national company of *Same Time, Next Year*, was cast as the colorful agent Blanche, with Greg Mullavey, Deborah May, and Holly Palance, who auditioned both in LA and New York cleverly wearing the same white dress so that we would remember her, completing the talented cast.

Since I had not met Mia and the rest of the cast did not know one another, an informal get-together was planned the night before rehearsals were about to begin. Mia did not show up, which, fearing that we had a temperamental movie actress on our hands, made me somewhat apprehensive.

The next morning we all assembled at the Minskov Theater. All except Mia. Twenty minutes after the appointed time she came through the door, with the apologetic explanation that she had walked into the wrong rehearsal room next door and had sat quietly in the corner trying to find a familiar face before her mistake became apparent. After being greeted with relieved smiles, she approached me and said, "Obviously, I'm a big fan of yours." The direct route to a playwright's heart. We began to read the play.

The reading went well and my only reservation about the script was that it seemed a beat too long. Written in a three-act form with two intermissions, it was constructed in a way that made it almost impossible for me to get it down to the ideal length. At one point during the run, Warren Crane, who was again our associate producer and stage manager, came to me and said, "Bern, there's a line in the play that says 'Nothing in life should last longer than two hours.'" I nodded. He said, "Well, we're running two hours and twenty minutes."

After the reading Mia, Tony, Carole, and I went to Joe Allen's restaurant to get to know one another better. This wasn't an easy job with Tony, and I don't think any of the cast ever got close to him. A complex man with an aloof demeanor, his obvious intelligence, mixed with a strong streak of paranoia, made him seem quite forbidding. Fortunately, this fit the character of Jason, who at one point says, "My own mother once said I lacked warmth."

At that first lunch, he felt compelled to announce that he was extremely cheap. This was true, and he was always terrified that he would have to pick up a restaurant check. When we were in Boston a restauranteur invited the entire company to have dinner at his expense. Even though I assured Tony that none of us would be presented with the check, as soon as coffee was served, he bolted from the restaurant.

Another facet of Tony's multifaceted personality was that he was a physical exhibitionist, and I always seemed to be having conversations with him when he was stark naked. All these quirks didn't make for an easygoing relationship and, although we didn't dislike each other, I was never really relaxed around him.

Although Mia wasn't exactly the "girl next door," she had none of the trappings one expects from a Hollywood-raised actress with a movie star and a famous director as parents and, during the year she was with the play, never displayed one bit of temperament. She had no problem with Tony taking first billing and graciously allowed him the stage-level dressing room he demanded, even though it was traditionally reserved for the female star. Despite her limited background in the theater, she fit in comfortably with the rest of the company, who, apart from Tony, quickly established a camaraderie and became a "merry band of players."

The rehearsals proceeded uneventfully, except for the odd time when Tony would come to work and offer quite astounding suggestions like, "Why don't we play this as if Leo and I have had a love affair in the past?" We quickly surmised that those ideas had come to him the night before when he had been smoking very strong hash.

We did hit one snag towards the end of rehearsals, when I watched the first run-through and was dumbfounded to see everything played in the mannered fashion of a Restoration comedy. I learned that Joe had advised the cast that the play was like an Oscar Wilde comedy and that every line should be given its full epigrammatic worth. I quickly disabused everyone of this notion and the next run-through, played at a normal pace, restored my shaky nerves.

The company, now with the addition of three understudies, arrived in Boston in perfect, crisp autumn weather, and most of us got settled into the now pleasantly familiar Ritz Carlton Hotel. We didn't see much of Tony away from the theater, but the rest of us ate together almost every night after the show in the chic cafe of the hotel. Some three weeks later Carole Cook, a flamboyant Texas-born redhead with a flair for comedy, was just ahead of me as we were checking out of the hotel. Presented with the hefty bill, she casually said to the very proper desk clerk, "I see. While I was here the suite turned into a condominium and I bought it, right? I mean, my relatives can come and use it next summer, right?" The clerk just looked puzzled.

I had some trepidation about the reception of the play as I wasn't sure if audiences were buying "charm" anymore, but our opening night audience at the Colonial Theater was very appreciative, the reviews were good, and we settled into a three-week run. I enjoyed watching *Romantic Comedy* the most of all my plays, not because I thought it was the best written but, partly, because with an absolutely perfect set by Douglas W. Schmidt and costumes by Jane Greenwood, it was visually the most beautiful. The cast were all extremely attractive and presented the play in a style very close to the way I had envisioned—an unusual occurrence because a playwright always has the perfect production in his head that is usually impossible to realize. The added enjoyment of the play for me was that it used the theater world as a background and, since it dealt with two playwrights, it allowed me to use dialogue in a special way, which Tony and Mia delivered impeccably.

One of the reasons I could watch *Romantic Comedy* without wincing over a longer period than my other plays was that, until much later in the run, when Tony's performance became quite eccentric, the production changed less than with other plays. The changes that occur in a play's presentation are the bane of all playwrights and I have found that, without exception, the performances early on are superior to any that follow. This is not because actors deliberately sabotage a play but because they truly believe they are "growing in a part." They are invariably wrong.

Unfortunately, the plans for a director to call a rehearsal to "take out the improvements" are not realistic because, even though a director's contract calls for him to check up on a production once a month, it has been my experience that it almost never happens. Directors don't like coming back to see a show once it has been launched because, by then, they are no longer a "father figure" to the actors, who are so independent they no longer want to even hear any notes; so, understandably, directors avoid the situation. As a playwright fortunate in having had a number of long runs, I am usually quite happy to see a replacement cast come in after six months or so.

We transferred to one of my favorite houses in New York, the Ethel Barrymore Theater, where, during the dress rehearsal, we encountered an unusual problem. At one point in the play, the character of Jason is supposed to be naked, but I had written it so that the actor was masked by a massage table, allowing him to wear undershorts. However, Tony had elected to play the scene actually nude, which in the large Colonial Theater was not a problem. However, in the smaller Barrymore Theater, which did not have the added distance of an orchestra pit, it was discovered that, even with his back to the audience, they could see his balls. An earnest exchange between Joe and I took place. "Maybe we could adjust the lighting," he said. I said, "Look, can't he black them out with makeup?" Joe said, "No, then all we'd have are two large *brown* balls. Even worse."

I have forgotten how this "costume problem" was solved, but Tony's nudity remained, and I remember overhearing the following exchange between two expensively dressed old ladies as they left the theater: "Did you like it, Evelyn?" "Yes, I did, but you know the problem?" "What?" "He's too fucking skinny!"

This was my third Broadway play and, although not immune to the terrors of opening nights, I must have developed a certain pragmatism because, while listening to the play on the backstage Tannoy in Mia's reception area outside her dressing room, I fell fast asleep. I invariably do this during the takeoff of an airplane, believing that everything's out of my hands and there's nothing I can do, and I must have had the same feeling during the opening performance. I awoke to see Mia in what I thought was the wrong costume. I leapt to my feet to tell her and she informed me that she was just about to play the last scene of the play.

The *Times* review was negative, but Clive Barnes's notice in the *Post*, along with the TV reviews, were all raves, and bolstered by a wonderful column in the *Washington Post*, we settled into a respectable run of close to a year.

Towards the end of the run Mia was hospitalized with an illness and missed about five weeks of performances. Morton chose to keep this a secret and so every night the part of Phoebe was played by an understudy who, because every audience thought this was her first performance, invariably received a standing ovation. This riled Tony, who one day appeared in Morton's office to demand that the understudy's name go up outside the theater, as her "unfair" curtain call reactions were causing him great discomfort. I guess he thought it was the sort of thing that gave standing ovations a bad name.

Tony never missed a performance but one day came down with the flu and took an extremely strong pill to ward off the symptoms. This had the effect of mentally putting him on another planet. At one point he had to give a crying Phoebe his handkerchief to dry her tears, but he had forgotten the prop and seriously offered her the tail of his shirt instead. To make matters even more ludicrous, a few minutes later, when talking about this character's lack of spontaneity, he was supposed to say, "A few minutes ago I almost didn't offer you my handkerchief." Instead he said, "I almost didn't offer you my shirt tail." Mia said that to avoid collapsing with laughter she thought of images of dead babies.

Jill and I as we looked when we played in *Same Time, Next Year* at the Citadel Theatre in Edmonton. Do I have a bald spot?

Christmas in England, circa 1986.

Barbara Hamilton, Gordon Pinsent, Charmion King, and me celebrating
Thanksgiving in Toronto.

Norman Lloyd, actor, producer, director, and tennis player extraordinaire, at opening of *Same Time Another Year* in Pasadena.

Elwy Yost, ebullient as always, in our beach house.

Tamas Szirtes, Hungarian director, in our London flat. "All we have to worry about is the mouse."

My sister and her husband, John. "It's funny, we know someone who thinks he is a poached egg."

Warren Crane, stage manager supreme of all my Broadway plays.

Pauline Collins (also known as Shirley Valentine) in a pensive mood.

Simon Callow—actor, writer, director, restaurant critic, and lover of life—in a rare moment of inactivity.

Stan Daniels at the piano, liking something he wrote.

Murray Neidorf, my business manager. "There will be enough pain. Better you should be comfortable."

The living room of our house in Beverly Hills. All our houses looked like sets for a romantic comedy.

In our London flat about a week before my encounter with the parrot.

A family portrait at the beach house.

The family at Christopher's graduation from Sarah Lawrence College.

On holiday in Dorset with John Alderton, Pauline Collins, and Peter Egan. We thought we were hiring a mini-van and got a seventeen-seat bus.

One of my favorite photos of Laurie.

The mishmash I saw made me quite sad as it is a favorite script of mine and should have been treated better. I had done the screenplay myself, but even if not a word is changed the work can be miscast or its tone and tempo can be incorrect, so that the original intention of the writer is never realized. Once again, nobody in the film was even close to being as good as the actors in the Broadway production.

The surgery I underwent at this time was for a chronic bad back ... my wife said that the migraines were gradually working their way down my body. I only mention this event because, a day or so after the surgery (which was completely successful), the anesthesiologist came to see me in my hospital room and asked me if I was a professional athlete. I said, "No, why do you ask?" He said, "Because just before you went under, you said, 'Be very careful ... I have about three more plays in me yet.'"

Actually, I had more, but my suffering with a herniated disc was to play a part in my next play, *Special Occasions*.

★ Yes, but can you bite down?

I was only half-joking when I vowed never to write a two-character play again because the cast parties were no fun. I embarked upon *Special Occasions* for the usual reason: I had an idea. The play was about a couple who split up after their fifteenth anniversary party. She stays in Los Angeles, he moves to New York, but over the next fourteen years they are brought together by the special occasions of high-school graduations, a funeral, her wedding, a child's accident, etc., and slowly manage to reframe their relationship. The idea was prompted by Jill, who was working as a psychotherapist at the time. Her marriage counseling sessions suggested to her that often spouses want their partners to be a certain way, but they only change when they divorce and marry someone else. In other words, they can change but not while with each other.

There was also an incident in our lives that was a factor in the creation of the play. We had offered our house for a high-school graduation party for the faculty, the students, and their parents. Since there were about fifteen teachers and thirty students, with two parents each, we figured we should provide food for about a hundred and five people. Close to two hundred people showed up. Most of the students had four parents, some six. It was a graphic demonstration of the debris of relationships left in the wake of multiple marriages, and I believed it was worth exploring.

The writing of *Special Occasions* was more difficult than my other plays as I had just given up smoking ... again. A cigarette smoker for twenty years, I had succumbed in the late sixties to the entreaties of my family and switched to pipe smoking. Pipes are wonderful "props" for writers as they come with all sorts of accessories like tamps, cleaners, and various brands of tobacco, providing a physical activity that soothes nerves and relieves the monotony of long hours at the desk. There's nothing like rewarding oneself with some contemplative puffs after a just-completed scene still considered brilliant. Over the years I had amassed a collection of very expensive pipes that I regarded not only as close friends, but as indispensable aids to putting words on paper. But I finally had to admit that my previous life as a cigarette smoker had caused me to gradually fall into the distressing habit of inhaling the smoke. One day, while working at our beach house, I decided to quit, went to the beach, and in a grand gesture (after all, I do work in the theater) threw all my pipes into the ocean. Feeling quite virtuous, I retreated to the deck of the beach house to bask in the strength of my character.

But I'd forgotten one thing—pipes are made of wood—and the tide floated them all back onto the shore. Two men, strolling on the beach, stopped as they came upon a garland of expensive straight-grained Dunhill pipes strewn on the sand. They both peered out at the ocean, I assume believing that there was a "pipe shipwreck" out there. Then they happily gathered up the treasure while I ducked down on the deck, not wanting to be identified as the idiot who had dispensed with a small fortune in pipes. As they trudged off down the beach, their pockets bulging, I had an intense desire for a cigarette.

But I persevered ... both with the play and with the not smoking. A postscript to this story: after four years of abstaining I understood how addictive tobacco can be. I was waiting in a restaurant and noticed an absolutely stunning woman light up a cigarette and realized I wanted the cigarette more than I wanted her. I eventually went back to pipe smoking, but this time I didn't inhale. Honestly.

I have never been able to ascertain whether Morton agreed to produce *Special Occasions* because he genuinely liked it, out of loyalty to me, or because I'd had three hits in a row and he didn't want to miss out on the chance that I'd have a fourth. Whatever the reason, we sent the script to Gene Saks, who agreed to direct, and set about trying to cast it. I don't remember all the actors we considered but do recall some meetings with Mary Tyler Moore. I also remember that Marlo Thomas had agreed to do the play only to phone me some weeks later to invite me to her apartment to tell me she had changed her mind. I have no idea why but suspect that she had sought advice from a group of friends, some of whom had advised her to back out. Gene had never been keen on the idea of Marlo playing the part so was not unduly concerned. We subsequently signed Suzanne Pleschette and Richard Mulligan.

All my previous plays had been written to be performed as one set, but the story of *Special Occasions* called for a number of locations. I thought this could be achieved as a simple, nonrealistic set. However, after we contracted David Jenkins to design the show, he suggested using three turntables to speed the changing of multiple sets. When I revealed my trepidation about using turntables because of the noise they created and their unreliability, he reassured me with the explanation that the modern revolves had none of these problems. Gene and I sat transfixed as he demonstrated on a model by pushing buttons that made the turntables spin noiselessly around. We agreed to go ahead with that design. And with such decisions flops are born.

Our rehearsals were once again at the Minskov rehearsal halls, but this time we were not scheduled to go out of town. Instead, we were but to move down the street to the Music Box, long considered to be one of the best theaters in New York, and play three weeks of previews before opening on February 7. I don't know why it was decided we should not go out of town—perhaps it was because of our complicated set—but it was our second bad decision.

Gene worked slowly, constantly changing his mind about the blocking, and rehearsals plodded along, and not helped by Suzanne's slowness in memorizing her lines, which, because of her long absence from the stage, made me apprehensive. It seemed that an inordinate amount of time was spent on Suzanne's wardrobe, which seemed to be the main focus of her attention. All the run-throughs in the rehearsal space were extremely ragged.

When I approached the theater on the day of our first technical rehearsal I was greeted by the sight of furniture spilling out onto Forty-Fifth Street. They couldn't get it all into the theater! I later watched the turntables shuddering around, making horrific ratchety sounds. To cover this noise I subsequently put in so much music that after one of the previews I overheard one woman say to her husband, "I loved the score." We found we didn't have enough stagehands to change all the furniture fast enough and eventually ended up with over twenty on the crew—this for a two-character play.

During the first few previews some major problems surfaced: Suzanne was pausing for a minisecond before each of her lines, imposing a deadly pace. Richard, an experienced stage actor, was conscious of this and, in trying to move the play along, was pushing so much that it was hurting his own performance. Suzanne has a deep, throaty voice, which is very effective on film, but in the theater it tends to rumble and lose clarity. On top of this, she was beginning to show signs of nerves, refusing to take any more notes from Gene. Now, Gene does tend to give extensive notes, with some of these sessions seeming to last as long as the play, but having a leading lady lock her door against the director doesn't bode well for a production. It also became apparent that there was no sexual chemistry between our two stars. Nobody's fault, just an unfortunate theatrical fact.

None of the portents were good, and to make matters worse, our box office was being hurt by the absolutely freezing weather. One night, on my way home to my apartment on Park Avenue, I encountered a hooker who, on previous nights, had always made overtures like, "Hi honey, want to party?" This night she was hugging herself as she hopped from one foot to another and greeted me with, "Honey, let's get a *room!*"

The previews staggered along. They were wildly erratic, with abysmal shows followed by quite good ones, which would send our hopes soaring only to be dashed by the next turgid presentation. I took to pacing in the basement below the stage, trying to rationalize what was happening by telling myself that I'd had three hits, I was due for a flop. It was small consolation that in *Romantic Comedy* I'd written about a playwright living through a flop and seemed to have captured the experience perfectly.

This book is intended to be a lighthearted reminiscence, but it's difficult to find anything funny about a failure in the theater—the memory still hurts—but I did have one curious experience. The actress Marion Seldes had been appearing in *Deathtrap* since the beginning of its long run. When we moved into the Music Box we bumped that show out and it moved to a theater a few blocks away. One night, feeling thoroughly depressed, I looked across the gloomy basement and saw the ghost of Marion Seldes glide across the space and up the stairs towards her old dressing room. My first reaction was that I must be really cracking up. I knew it couldn't be Marion herself as she was still appearing in *Deathtrap* in another theater, so it had to be her ghost. I went upstairs, sidled up to Warren Crane, who was running the show, and said, "I think I'm having a breakdown. I just saw the ghost of Marion Seldes downstairs." He glanced up from the board and said, "No, it was Marion. She's not in the second act of her show, so she came down to watch a couple of scenes before she went back for her curtain call."

By now, in 1982, the critics' attendances were staggered over three previews, and I thought the performances they saw were among our best, so I began to think we might just pull it off. It was not to be.

The morning after the opening night Morton decided to close the show. We didn't have all the reviews, but I gathered that the *Times* notice was devastating and this, combined with no sizeable advance, sealed our fate. At the time I accepted this decision without question, but, upon reflection, I think that because of the positive audience reaction and the favorable TV reviews we learned about later, we should have tried to make a run for it. Probably wishful thinking.

When the postmortem was concluded I walked to the theater to meet Richard and Suzanne. I felt most sorry for Richard, who had moved to New York with his wife with the hopes of a long run. He stayed on for a few days at a hotel across the street, where he was subjected to the depressing sight of the set being taken out. Suzanne, who apparently had come off well in the reviews, seemed happy to be going back to Beverly Hills and her movie-of-the-week jobs. She had received so many opening night flowers that they overflowed from her dressing room and down the outside stairs, and she offered them to anyone who wanted them. I grabbed a couple of plants, piled into a cab, and, festooned with foliage, went home.

Still holding the plants, I entered our apartment and told Jill we were closing. She immediately burst into tears. Her explanation was, "Someone has to cry over that play." I was still too stunned to react that strongly but later that day was hit by a wave of melancholy, not simply because my play had flopped but because of a nagging suspicion that I was one of the architects of its failure.

That night Jill woke up at 3 A.M. to find me in the living room scribbling on a yellow legal pad. When she asked what I was doing I told her I was making some notes about how we *should* have done the play. She thought for a moment and then said, "Well, that's very healthy—I guess."

Jill left (escaped?) to visit some friends in the Bahamas the next morning, but I was trapped in town by some ongoing dental work. I kept to myself, preferring to lick my wounds in private, and ruminated over the adage that it takes three years to do a Broadway play: one to write it, one to get it on, and one to get over it. I had not read the *Times* review but noticed that the usually loquacious elevator operators in my building became strangely silent when I entered, so I assumed *they* had. I was probably being paranoid—I know I was afraid to open restaurant menus in case there was a bad review there—but a visit to my dentist helped put things in perspective. When he asked me how things were I said, "Well, the teeth are fine, but my play closed." He said, "Yes, I heard about that, but can you bite down?" I told him I could but that I wasn't sure I wanted to anymore.

After I got back to LA I resumed "normal" life, feeling I'd come through the whole experience relatively unscathed. I held onto this fiction for about six months. But when I sat down to start writing again I became aware of a feeling of dread in my stomach as I realized I was about to spend a year of my life on a project that would succeed or fail because of one man's opinion at the *New York Times*. For the first time in my life I became completely blocked. If you have read this far you will have gathered that I love the theater. There has only ever been one fly in the greasepaint—the critics. Of course, it is a waste of time railing against them, as they always have the last word. Peter Nichols, the British playwright, has capsulized this thought beautifully with the line, "It's feeding the hand that bites you." Nevertheless.

I am always skeptical of people in show business who state that they never read reviews. I think what they mean is that they never read *bad* reviews. I will devour good reviews. I will even read bad reviews—but not until a year or so after the production. By then I have made up such a scathing notice in my head nothing written on paper can possibly match it. "Witless"?—gee, that's not so bad. "Inane"?—we could practically use that in the ads.

I don't believe that reviewers fully realize how much an attack in print can damage a writer psychologically and am amazed when they defend their attack by saying, "It's not personal." Not personal? A writer spends a year or more trying to distill his life experiences into a viable evening in the theater; a reporter judges the work as worthless and really believes that the playwright is not going to take it personally? A bad review attacks the *most* personal aspects of any writer's life.

Critics reviewing comedy are doubly dangerous. Since most of them never display one iota of wit in their columns, their senses of humor are quite suspect. When a reviewer dismisses a comedy by saying, "It's funny but ..." I always want them to pause and dwell on that sentence for a moment, because funny is hard!

There's an old show business story about the marvelous character actor Edmund Gwenn, who was very sick in hospital. A friend visited him and asked how he was. Mr. Gwenn said, "I'm dying." The friend sympathetically said, "Yes, I know ... it must be very hard." Mr. Gwenn said, "No, dying is easy. Comedy is hard."

Comedy *is* hard ... even for people who know how to do it ... but for those who don't, it's impossible. That's why comedy writing is so difficult to teach. Oh, the mechanics—the element of surprise, where the key word should be in a feed or punch line, and how a joke should be constructed—can be passed on, but a comic sensibility is something one is either born with or develops very early. This talent must be blended with a gift for storytelling and creating characters who are identifiable, and that combination is quite rare.

Edna Ferber once said about life, "It's all velvet," meaning that it's all material that can one day be used, so memory is very important to a writer. Not just remembering specific incidents but idiosyncratic behavior that you find amusing. For instance, two of my oldest friends are the Canadian actors Charmion King and Gordon Pinsent. Many years ago I discovered that the one who is up first in the morning will scan the obituaries in the newspaper and, when the other appears, will say, "Guess who died today?" The other will then ask, "Was it a he? Was he in politics? Show business?" etc. This form of twenty questions is continued until the identity of the deceased is guessed. They claim it softens the blow. And yes, I did use this in a play.

It's important to remember your own foibles too, especially if they are embarrassing and make you look quite stupid, because human folly is the essence of comedy. One night at a party, while I was still living in Toronto, I was introduced to a group of people. One man misheard the introduction and thought that my name was Peter. I should have corrected him right away, but, thinking I'd never see him again, I let it go. But I did see him again. Not frequently but sometimes, as I was walking down the street, he would yell over from the other side, "How are you, Peter?" If alone, I would cheerfully yell back, "Fine!" but if I was with someone, they would invariably ask, "Why did he call you Peter?" I would then mumble, "He probably thinks I'm someone else." This went on for a number of years, but it was no big deal because our encounters were so rare. Then, one day, the man, who was a set designer, and I were assigned to the same show. At the first production meeting he kept calling me Peter, which really puzzled the rest of the staff. Finally, one asked, "Why do you keep calling him Peter?" The man said, "Because that's his name." Everyone looked at me to correct him. I mumbled, "Actually, it's not, it's Bernard." There was a long pause. "But I've been calling you Peter for fifteen years," he said. "I know, and I'm sorry. I should have told you, but the moment went by and then, when you kept calling me Peter, I was too embarrassed to correct you because I'd let it go on so long." He had no reply to this but looked at me as if I was a very peculiar fellow. Which I probably was ... and am.

I'm often asked how I know something is going to make people laugh. I don't, but I'm sometimes given a hint if I try out material at a dinner party. If people laugh in a dining room, they'll probably laugh in a theater. When relating something funny it's very important that you make sure you have the right audience. Paul Wayne, a friend of mine, suffered from debilitating migraines and was admitted to a hospital for some extensive tests. While he was sitting on the examination table with dozens of wires attached to his head, he said to the nurse, "Are you sure this is going to clear up my dandruff?" The nurse looked puzzled and said, "This is not for dandruff ... it's for migraines." When I related this to my mother, who also suffered from an "irony deficiency," she said, "Well, *did* he have dandruff?"

I'm always amazed that at awards times wonderful comedies that celebrate life in the most positive way are passed over in favor of the latest sensation-seeking drama. Why is this? Because comedy, when done well, *looks* easy and seems light and frivolous. Well, what's wrong with frivolous? I've always believed that laughter is the perfume of life—it makes life bearable. Please ... send in the clowns.

Usually critics are much harsher on playwrights than on actors or directors. My theory about this is that they don't have a clue about how a performance is created or how a play is directed, but since they make a living with words, they have the delusion that they could write a play themselves. Please, be my guest.

I've found that critics who like one's work at the beginning of one's career will, for the most part, always like it, or at least be favorably disposed. In my case, Clive Barnes, Martin Gottfried, and John Simon in the States and Sheridan Morley and Jack Tinker in England have always been supportive. As a theatergoer simply looking for a play to see, the critic I trust the most is John Simon, meaning that I generally agree with his opinions. He also writes more entertainingly than most, and I admire the fact that he is brave enough to voice opinions not "politically correct."

Anyway, there I was nursing my writer's block when something that is extremely rare in the theater occurred. I was given a second chance.

★ Second chance in London

Ray Cooney, the British playwright and producer, had either seen one of the New York performances of *Special Occasions* or had read the script and offered me the chance to direct a production of the play at the Ambassadors Theatre in London's West End. I had never actually directed before and had no ambitions in that area, but since I had a specific idea of how the play should be presented, I gratefully accepted. The project was made even more attractive a few days later when Pauline Collins and John Alderton agreed to perform in the play. The opening was scheduled for two months away, so I immediately flew to London for preproduction meetings.

The Ambassadors is one of the most intimate theaters in London and seemed perfect for the production I envisioned, which had a minimalistic set, a cyclorama, and a number of blocks that could become any piece of furniture we wanted. These could be moved by the actors, which meant we could dispense with stagehands. Effects could be enhanced by lighting and music. Props would also be minimal. Because of the style of the production, the actors could change costumes in full view of the audience. We could move the play along quickly with this device, giving it the almost filmic quality of one scene dissolving into another, unhampered by stage waits and grinding turntables.

While in London I was disappointed to learn that Pauline Collins would not be doing the play because of a lucrative film offer. We quickly cast Jan Waters. Partly because John's Yorkshire roots had left him with traces of a north-country accent, I decided to change the setting of the play to Manchester and London. Given my British background, this was not a difficult job.

I returned to London in November, rented a flat in Chelsea, and, while crossing Hyde Park in a taxi on the morning of our first rehearsal, gazed at the winter mist rising from the frozen grass and came to grips with the pleasant fact that I was on my way to direct my own play in the West End. Ever the romantic, it appealed to my sense of dramatic symmetry.

The luxury of being able to rehearse for four weeks on the stage where the play would be performed was somewhat offset by freezing temperatures inside the theater, forcing us to work bundled up in sweaters, scarves, and even gloves. Outside, the IRA was mounting a campaign of exploding bombs all over London, but, as is usual in the theater, our focus on the intensive rehearsal process made us almost oblivious to the rest of the world.

Perhaps because of the English tone of the play, and because the production bore no resemblance to the one in New York, I was able, for the most part, to divorce myself from the fact that I had written it. I found that, as the director, I was much more ruthless about cutting the text than when I had functioned solely as the writer. My main problem was that John and Jan worked at different paces. John came into rehearsals completely prepared, with his lines pretty well learned, while Jan was much more lackadaisical, and I had the feeling that once she left rehearsals she never looked at the script. She liked to rehearse a few lines at a time, repeating the process endlessly, and we quickly realized that she was using rehearsals to learn her lines. This really bothered John, and I was forced into the not unusual position for a director of being a conciliator between two actors.

I was sometimes amazed at the differences between American and British actors in the way they worked. One day, over lunch, knowing that Jan was divorced, I asked her about her relationship with her ex-husband. Very British, she said, "Why on earth would you want to know that?" I suggested that her feelings about her ex-husband might have some bearing on the situation in the play and might be useful as to the playing of her character. Her eyes widened, "Good Lord, I never thought of that. Yes, of course! How clever of you to have come up with that!" American actors gazing at their navels can be tedious, but perhaps there is a happy medium.

At the beginning of rehearsals John had asked me if I'd ever directed any of my own plays before. I faked a three-second pause to indicate that I was trying to remember and then said, "No, not my *own* plays," implying that I had directed hundreds of other writers' plays, including dozens at the Moscow Arts Theater. During our third week of rehearsals John and his wife Pauline came to dinner at our flat. While in the kitchen with Jill, John extolled my virtues as a director and expressed his amazement that I hadn't directed any of my own plays before. Jill, unable to lie except about Christmas surprises, blurted out, "He's never directed *any* plays before!" When John came out of the kitchen his face was a few shades paler than normal.

During rehearsals, a typical Anglo-American difference in attitudes about psychotherapy surfaced. John, in expressing his lack of understanding about a scene dealing with psychotherapy, said, "I've never known anyone who's been in analysis." I said, "I've never known anyone who hasn't." Not absolutely true—despite my wife's career as a psychotherapist I had stubbornly resisted treatment, although I suspect that she had subtly practiced on me at home.

Our previews seemed to go well, although we didn't play to full houses. Because of the small houses it was difficult to know how well the comedy was working. The British are quite ineffective when it comes to advertising or any public relations, believing it is bad form to be "pushy." When I complained to Ray Cooney about the lack of audiences, he told me that not even *The Mousetrap*, which was playing next door, was doing any business. I said, "They're in their thirty-second year—we're in our third *day*!" However, during the preview period I appreciated the calm atmosphere, which was in direct contrast to Broadway's smash-hit-or-bust philosophy. Even opening nights in Britain are low key, with few extravagant parties and an "It's only a play—we'll have a nice little run" attitude. I must admit, though, that after a while I did miss the highly charged Broadway atmosphere of everything depending on that opening night roll of the dice, when you found out whether the play was going to be assigned to oblivion or seen by millions around the world.

After the dress rehearsals another difference in cultural sensibilities arose. Ray Cooney, a nice, quintessential Englishman, told me, "You cannot have a man cry on the English stage." When I asked why, he said, "It embarrasses the audience." I said, "No, it only embarrasses you, Ray."

I believed the production was in pretty good shape and looked forward to the opening night. Because the play was being produced by the Theatre of Comedy, which was sponsored by practically every big star in England, we would be playing to a celebrity-packed audience. The morning of the opening night disaster came to visit.

It started with a phone call from John, who told me that his back had gone out and that he was having trouble even moving. I suggested he get to a physical therapist and then meet me at the theater. When I arrived I was greeted by the sight of a man bent almost double. An expert on bad backs by now, I told him there was no way he would be able to give a performance that night. John agreed but then came up with the astounding suggestion that he start the play, staying on the stage for as long as he could stand the pain, and then I take over! My reaction to this was an unequivocal "No way!" He said, "Why not? You know the lines." I pointed out that I only knew the lines well enough to shout them out in rehearsal when the actors dried and that the idea of my going on in the opening performance in the West End was ludicrous.

As the day progressed John's back got marginally better so that he was now walking at only a forty-five-degree angle, and he came up with another suggestion. This one was that before the opening curtain he should make a speech to the audience telling them what had happened so they wouldn't be surprised at the way he moved. This seemed to me like begging for sympathy, but he told me I wasn't as familiar with English audiences as he and that they would love it. Fifteen minutes before curtain time found me kneeling behind John, applying adhesive tape to his lower back and buttocks. I said, "Did Tyrone Guthrie start this way?"

When John appeared before the curtain wearing a silk dressing gown and a clenched face he looked like a young Noël Coward ... in extreme pain. He told the audience that he had "ricked" his back and not to worry if he couldn't bend to pick up props. He jokingly suggested that if his costume changes took too long that they should go into the bar for a drink. He also said that there was a scene in the play where the *character*'s back went out but that they shouldn't be concerned because that would be him *acting*. I stood at the back of the theater vowing that, in the future, I would only write for film and dreading the moment when John would hobble onstage.

At the beginning of *Special Occasions* the two characters make their entrance by waltzing onto the stage. The curtain rose, we heard the music, and John and Jan danced onto the set like Fred and Ginger. Not a sign of a bad back. The play progressed, with John fluidly moving around the stage. Gradually the audience began to murmur as people turned to each other and muttered, "What was that bad back speech about?" During the intermission I went backstage to find out what had affected this miraculous cure. John said, "It must have been Doctor Stage." In nontheatrical terms this meant the opening night adrenaline had banished the pain. At the end of the play John took his bow and then, when the curtain went down, fell to his knees and crawled to his dressing room. All the reviews mentioned the mysterious precurtain speech by the leading actor. To my knowledge, his back never went out again.

Generally, I was pleased with the production, but, because I am primarily a writer of comedy, I felt the play's melancholy quality worked against it becoming a smash hit. On the other hand, that quality is what many people liked best about the piece. My other reservation was that perhaps we had been *too* minimal with the sets and that the presentation had a stark feeling about it. Despite the fact that we never fully sold out, the play had "a nice little run" and was considered a minor success, giving it a new life and generating many other foreign productions.

The best production I saw was at the Madach Theater in Budapest, where the play was called *California Divorce* (they thought these two words were good for the box office) and ran for seven years in repertory. I felt the success of this show was largely due to the physical presentation that managed to find the perfect balance between the overproduction of Broadway and the underproduction of London. The couple who played it were married in real life, and this fact was utilized by stringing large blowups of happy events of their marriage across the top of the set. This added an effective bittersweet aura to the play.

Some years later, I was involved as the playwright (but not the director) in a production at the Pasadena Theater, where, despite the usual turntable problems, with them being physically pushed around one night, it played for eight weeks to appreciative audiences. In the theater, sometimes tenacity is more important than talent.

What's in a name?

By this time, in the mid-eighties, we had sold our house in Brentwood and moved to a large apartment at Seventy-First and Central Park West in New York. I had visions of doing one play a year just like the playwrights of the thirties. If you want to make God laugh just tell him your plans—I've never had another show on Broadway. I believe Noël Coward said something to the effect that "to have a long career in the theater one has to keep popping out of different holes"—so I started to explore different holes. I began to write a thriller called *Fatal Attraction*.

I had never been particularly interested in writing in that genre but concocted the play because of a desire to try something different, and for the more practical reason that I had a notion of how to murder someone in an unusual way. At least that's how I rationalized my decision at the time. In retrospect, I believe the truth is that after *Tribute* and *Special Occasions* I was leery of putting myself on the line again emotionally and, still gun shy from the New York reviews of my last play, I took refuge by writing something concerned more with craft than with personal conviction.

The genesis for the play was an incident in a Jacuzzi at our Malibu beach house that was hidden under a sliding floor. One day the button that controlled the sliding top was inadvertently pushed and the occupant was almost trapped in the boiling water under the floor. I was also interested in featuring a character who was so appealing the audience would fall in love with her only to eventually learn she had murdered three people. This notion was prompted by an observation that, usually, whenever a good person who turned out to be evil was presented theatrically, the audience quickly sensed a dark side to the character long before the denouement. I wanted the leading woman, Blair Griffin, to be absolutely adorable even if it meant risking the ire of the audience when they learned the truth.

I reread all the major mystery thrillers: Emlyn Williams's *Night Must Fall*, Anthony Shaeffer's *Sleuth*, Agatha Christie's *Witness for the Prosecution* and *Ten Little Indians*, Ira Levin's *Deathtrap*, Patrick Hamilton's *Angel Street*, and, perhaps my favorite, *Dial M for Murder* by Frederick Knott. To digress for a moment, my friend, the television mystery writer Richard Levinson, a cocreator of the series *Columbo*, once told me that he was introduced to Frederick Knott and smugly said, "You know there's a loophole in *Dial M for Murder*." Without batting an eye, Mr. Knott said, "Actually, there are three." Dick spent days trying to discover the other two before he realized he'd been had.

The difficulty of the form is perhaps best demonstrated by the fact that, despite the thousands of mysteries written for the stage, only about a dozen have survived the years to become classics of the genre. Writing a thriller is very much like putting an intricate puzzle together, and it became like a mind-bending game as, over a period of months, I gradually worked out how to commit a perfect crime. Once this was accomplished I had to address the equally difficult task of working out how a detective solved the murder.

Morton Gottlieb was no longer actively involved in the theater, and thrillers were out of fashion on Broadway, so with no New York producer panting to read the script, the play languished on the shelf for some time. Then in 1984 it was read by someone at the St. Lawrence Centre Theatre in Toronto and I was offered a production. Tom Troupe was signed to direct and we embarked on a series of auditions in search of the right cast.

Ken Howard was cast as the male lead, Gus Braden, but the part of Blair Griffin, who is a waiflike child-woman, was more difficult to fill. We eventually settled on an actress whose experience was mainly in television but who had all the right physical attributes the part required. I am not going to reveal her name as she is still working and I don't want the recounting of the following experience to impact on her career. Let's call her Sheila.

The rehearsals took place in Toronto and, almost immediately, I sensed we might be in trouble. Actors work in different ways, some more slowly than others, but our problem was that Sheila was not showing us even a glimmer of the character. Also, her voice was so small that, even in the confined rehearsal room, nobody could hear her. I became even more apprehensive when I learned that she had been let go from two major productions in the past. Tom offered to work with her at night, but ten days into rehearsal we saw no improvement. It wasn't that she was working with her own method but that she had *no* method. Ken Howard, who was going to be brilliant in his part, kept his counsel until one day when I tried to reassure him by saying, "Ken, I know you're worried about Sheila's performance, but Tom is working with her and I'm sure she'll be fine by the opening." He said, "Look, I wasn't going to say anything but since you've brought it up—you're not going to open with this actress. I'm willing to go on rehearsing with her, but, believe me, she won't open in the show. And if she does, you'll never see your play—and that's what we're here for, isn't it?" After this chilling speech he walked away, leaving me with the unpleasant realization that we were going to have to replace an actor—something we'd never had to do before in any of my plays.

I offered to accompany Tom that night to break the news to Sheila, but, because he was closer to her than any of us, he thought it would be better coming from him alone. We were all staying in the same hotel, and when he came down to my room he said the encounter had been a devastating experience. I asked, "Did she cry?" Tom, a sensitive soul, said, "No, but I did."

We were now faced with an opening ten days away with no leading lady and we stayed up racking our brains for possible replacements. The tension and our exhaustion sometimes made us giddy and, as the evening wore on, our desperation, which produced some outlandish casting suggestions, frequently reduced us to helpless laughter. In the middle of one of these fits of hysteria Tom froze and wordlessly pointed to an envelope that had appeared under the door. It contained a note from Sheila. I don't remember what she had written, but Tom looked absolutely stricken. When I asked why the color had disappeared from his face he said, "She must have heard us!" Bewildered I said, "Heard what?" He said, "We were *laughing*! She must have thought we were laughing at *her*!" I tried to make him feel better with the logic that the note had probably been delivered by a bellboy, but he wouldn't listen and insisted on going out into the corridor, closing the door, and asking me to say something inside the room. Feeling completely foolish, I loudly said, "Well, I'm certainly glad to see the back of that bitch!" The door was flung open and Tom yelled, "I heard every word!" I pointed out that nobody had actually said that, but he wouldn't be comforted and stewed about it for days.

A few days later Sheila wrote me a letter protesting her dismissal and insisting she would have been ready for opening night. Although the letter was understandably strident and accusatory in tone I sympathized with her and felt compelled to answer her with a reasoned explanation of our actions. She, in turn, wrote back, this time in a more conciliatory manner and I thought, "My God,

I've found a pen pal." Some months later, at a book signing in LA for a mutual friend, Tom spotted Sheila and crouched on the floor, hiding behind a stack of books. She and I talked in a friendly manner and she told me that my letter had helped soothe her feelings but that she still believed that we had been wrong. Well, we'll never know.

Dawn Wells, best known for her long stint in the TV series *Gilligan's Island*, generously agreed to replace Sheila without even reading the script. I had never met her, although she had appeared in a touring production of *Romantic Comedy* in which Tom had also appeared. When I asked how old she was, Tom, always vague about ages, said, "About thirty-eight," which was stretching the character's age but still in the realm of believability. The day Dawn was due to arrive there was a blurb in *People* magazine, which has the charming habit of printing everyone's age, that said, "Dawn Wells, aged fifty-one." She did look much younger, and her age didn't present a problem. Very competent (and I mean this in the best sense), willing, and hard working, she saved our necks and it is no reflection on her abilities that she just wasn't right for the part, which was written very specifically and called for certain qualities hard to find.

The setting for the play was a two-story house on Nantucket and was superbly designed by Gerry Hariton and Vicki Baral, with a floor that slid open to reveal a steaming Jacuzzi that never failed to get an audible reaction from the audience. During the previews the audience screamed at three designated spots in the play and literally came out of their seats. We spent some time adjusting the blocking to ensure that they all screamed as one. I found it was very similar to dealing with laughs and instructed the actors, "Don't move on the scream!"

There were other vocal reactions that were not as welcome. Some of the audience, embarrassed at their screaming, would lapse into tension-relieving laughter. The main problem was in the second act, where I had gone overboard in trying for horrific effects and I realized the play needed some rewriting. Since the rewrite was fairly major, I flew back to New York and returned two days later to put in the changes that quelled the unwanted laughs.

Before the opening night performance Tom and I were going up in the hotel elevator and I casually remarked that Barbara and Wayne, the aforementioned murderer who had allegedly killed his wife with a candlestick, were coming to the show. Tom, always the worrier, said, "My God, there are murders and knives in the play! What will he think?" At this point, he got off at his floor and just as the elevator doors were closing I jokingly said, "And what about the candlesticks on the set?" As I entered my room the phone was already ringing. It was Tom who wanted to remove all the candlesticks from the set. I talked him out of it.

The production received the mixed reviews typical of Toronto critics when judging the work of a native son, but the word of mouth was excellent and we broke the house record with a sold-out run. The play was also optioned by Duncan Weldon, one of London's most successful producers.

While waiting for the London rehearsals of *Fatal Attraction* to start I wrote the first draft of *Return Engagements*, a comedy set in Stratford, Ontario. The play's series of interlocking vignettes enabled me to use some interesting incidents I had been carrying around in my head for a number of years and also employ a time frame to create eight colorful characters, who all age thirty years during the course of the play. It was optioned for Broadway, but it was decided that this kind of light comedy could only succeed in New York with four major stars in the cast. We managed to interest four stars, but they were never available at the same time so, after many frustrating months, I reluctantly shelved the project.

The London production of *Fatal Attraction* was directed by David Gilmore, with the two leads played by Susannah York and Denis Quilley. Susannah was also a bit mature for the part and didn't help matters by never being absolutely certain of her lines even after playing the part for some weeks. Denis, who was marvelous as Gus Braden, did double duty by constantly putting her back on track with whispered cues and quick-thinking adjustments in the text.

This inability or laziness of actors to learn lines as written is a major complaint of all playwrights, who find it hard to forgive them as they mangle lines the writer has spent months, or even years, composing. A playwright I know who possesses a mordant wit once cast an old friend (whom we will call George) in a play and then suffered through rehearsals as the actor paraphrased every line in his part. Eventually, the actor had to be fired, completely rupturing the long relationship the two men had enjoyed. Some six months later, the playwright told me that George's wife had died. I inquired whether he had contacted the actor, and when he nodded I asked if he had spoken to him for very long. The playwright said, "Just long enough for him to paraphrase his wife's dying words."

We opened at the Yvonne Arnaud Theatre in Guildford and then transferred into the Royal Haymarket, one of the most beautiful theaters in London. At the time I was delighted to have a play in this theater but have since reflected that the prestigious house may have somewhat overwhelmed our "nice little thriller" and that we may have had a longer run in a Shaftesbury Avenue theater.

Jill and I decided not to put ourselves through the experience of another nerve-wracking opening night and took the eminently sane action of watching the curtain go up and then repairing to the Savoy Grille for a quiet dinner. I recommend this plan to all playwrights.

We had a respectable run at the Haymarket while a revival of *Same Time, Next Year*, starring Dennis Waterman and Rula Lenska, was playing simultaneously at the Old Vic Theatre, so my experience of having two plays on Broadway at the same time was repeated in London.

I am often asked whether the movie *Fatal Attraction* is based on my play. It is not. The title? Well, that's a different story. Make of it what you will.

First of all, my play preceded the movie by a number of years. While the play was still running in London I had a meeting with Sherry Lansing and her partner Stanley Jaffe to pitch an idea for a movie called *Sabbatical*. They liked the idea and commissioned me to write the script. After the formal part of the meeting was over I was asked what I had been doing lately and told them I had a play running in London called *Fatal Attraction*. "What a great title," they said. They mentioned they were in preproduction of a thriller called *Diversions* but would like to read my script. I gave them a copy, and was told over the phone that they liked it and would deliver it by mail. This they did but, oddly, with no covering letter. I went off to London to write the first draft of *Sabbatical*.

When I returned to New York I phoned Sherry Lansing, who was on the set of a movie they were shooting. The phone was answered with, "*Fatal Attraction*—production." Of course, I was flabbergasted. When I confronted Sherry Lansing she said they got the title from "somewhere else." I offered to come up with another title, but she said that they really liked "Fatal Attraction." Now, I am not litigious by nature and, at the time, also thought that a title was not protected. I later learned that I was only half right and that infringement upon a title of a play running in London that had not been produced yet in the United States certainly could be actionable. Also, I believed that, like most movies, it would come and go quickly and not have any impact upon my play. Anyway, I didn't want to dwell on an unpleasant situation and simply told my film agent, Norman Kurland, to return the advance money for

Sabbatical as I didn't want to be in business with anyone I suspected of situational ethics. He agreed with my position, followed my wishes, and I believed the matter was closed.

Not quite. The galling aftermath is that I am frequently contacted by producers who want to do *Fatal Attraction* but don't want to seem as if they are ripping off the title of the film. I suggested another title, so it is often produced as *Concerto for Murder*.

Oddly enough, the play has had great success in Germany under the title *Do Not Eat Poisoned Strawberries*. Oh well, what's in a name?

★ The British Museum loses its charm ★

At this point I had long stopped writing plays for monetary reasons (I'm not sure I ever had) and was not even writing because of a burning urge to artistically express myself. I still enjoyed the act of writing but was aware that my personality was more that of a gregarious actor than a solitary writer, and I realized that my primary reason for putting words on paper was that I needed the action and social interplay of rehearsals. *An Act of the Imagination* was written out of this desire for companionship. I also had an idea.

The play deals with a shy, absent-minded middle-aged author who usually writes mystery books but who is about to publish a love story, complete with steamy sex scenes, about a man having an affair with a passionate Welsh girl. Then, in the play, a girl shows up and claims she is the girl in the book. She has some credentials to back her up; she speaks Welsh and knows some intimate details about the author. The author insists that he has never seen the girl in his life and his wife believes him. Then the girl is found murdered. Act Two serves up many more twists and turns, and at the end of the play we are not sure if what we have been watching actually happened or if they were all "an act of the imagination."

I secluded myself in my den (my wife claimed it was to escape the frantic preparations that were taking place for our son's wedding) and emerged ten days later with a completed first draft. This short span of time was not as surprising as it may sound as, once I actually start writing, I usually finish a first draft in under a month. The "thinking time" that precedes the writing, though, can be anywhere from six months to twenty years. Not all of this is conscious, but more a matter of an idea gestating subconsciously until it is ready to write.

I had set the play in London, not only because I thought it had an English "feel" to it, but also because I believed that British audiences responded well to mysteries and that it would be easier to get a production there. I mailed the script to Duncan Weldon, who immediately phoned me with plans to open the play in Guildford two months later and then tour it to Brighton and Croydon, with an eye to then bring it into London.

The experience was almost entirely joyless. When I arrived in London I met with the director, Val May, who suggested some revisions that would entail a complete rewrite of the second act. His feeling was that the play should be more of a psychological drama than a mystery and that the changes would give the piece more weight. Now, I am quite capable of digging in my heels to protect my work, but since none of his suggestions were absurd and because I had written the play so quickly and so recently and was still unsure of its merits, I agreed to make the changes. Two weeks of frantically rewriting the play, now retitled *Sweet William*, not only destroyed any objectivity I had about the work but filled me with a clammy apprehension about the approaching rehearsals.

This state of mind probably triggered an odd reaction in me to the following incident. One drizzly London summer morning I was sitting in the almost deserted Comedy Theatre watching auditions for the supporting roles. An actress, who was about forty years too mature for the part, had been hired to read the already cast leading lady role with the auditioning actors. To my jaundiced ears she sounded a lot like Dame Edith Evans (but without the talent), and as I watched a string of poor actors, totally unfamiliar with the play, stumble through the brief scenes they had been handed I was suddenly struck by the bizarre way I had chosen to make a living. In essence, this consisted of sitting in a room to put figments of my imagination on paper, people being hired to pretend to be these fantasy creatures, and other people paying money to come and watch these impersonators act out this imaginary tale. The fact that *An Act of the Imagination* dealt with unreality versus reality heightened my sense of having stepped through the "looking glass," and I resolved in the future to spend more of my time in the "real world." Remnants of this feeling are still with me.

When I watched the opening night performance I could see that the new version of the play made sense and that the attentive audience liked it. But *I* didn't like it. It wasn't that it was bad, simply that the rather earnest psychological drama up on the stage had nothing to do with my original intention of creating an exciting theatrical mystery. The production subsequently enjoyed a successful tour, but I did not want Duncan to bring it into the West End and flew back to the States having learned to place more trust in my first creative instincts. Samuel French has since published the play under the title *An Act of the Imagination* with my original draft intact.

A rereading of *Return Engagements* convinced me that the play merited a production somewhere so, after rewriting it for eight actors instead of four, I mailed it off to various theaters around the country. Two weeks after this, my European agent, Elisabeth Marton, who had always admired the play, arranged for a German-language production in Hanover, which was soon followed by a South American run, where the play was called *Souffle*. Shortly after I was offered a summer tour of New England theaters.

The idea of the tour appealed to me because going back to summer stock seemed a pleasant way of completing one of the circles of my life. Tom Troupe, who was to direct the production, and I set up some audition sessions in New York. We were seeing dozens of actors, each audition about fifteen minutes apart, and by the middle of the afternoon of the third day we were both groggy from the frantic pace of the readings. At this point, a chimpanzee, fully dressed in a suit and smoking a cigar, entered, sat down opposite us, and offered us a sip of coffee from the cup he was carrying. Now, I still don't know why he was there—I suppose his trainer had brought him to the building on other business and, on a whim, had sent him in to see us. We were too stunned to comment on his presence and when he got up and left the room we didn't have a chance to talk about it as another actor came in, quickly followed every quarter hour by a procession of other auditionees. That night, while walking up Central Park West, Tom stopped, turned to me with a puzzled expression, and said, "Wait a minute—am I crazy or did an *ape* come into the office this afternoon?" The experience had not lodged in my mind either, so I thought for a moment before I slowly said, "No, I believe it was a chimp—but he wasn't right for the part!"

We eventually assembled a cast willing to work for less than their normal salaries in exchange for the adventure of putting on a new play in the three best summer theaters in America. The group consisted of David Hedison, Louise Sorrell, Ben Mittelman, Mia Dillon, Jill Larsen, Reed Birney, Marsha Waterbury, and Tom Troupe. With the exception of Mia Dillon, all were old friends with whom I had previously worked, and the experience did evoke the carefree summers of my youth. We had fun, and the tour, although not without the usual tension of a first production, validated my faith that the play could provide an amusing evening at the theater.

The genesis of my next play, *I Remember You*, was an incident that occurred when I was in London in 1993. When I had immigrated as a teenager to Canada in 1948 I had bid an emotional good-bye to my first love, a girl named Wendy. Some forty years later, while walking on the Aldwych, I saw a girl who looked exactly as Wendy had when she was eighteen. The likeness was so striking that I followed her but lost her in the crowd on the Strand. Out of this came a play in which a man falls in love with the same face twice but doesn't know that the second girl is the daughter of his first love. Because of the light romantic tone of the play I thought it would be enhanced by music, and so I made the leading man a cocktail pianist and indulged in my love of American standard songs of the thirties and forties to counterpoint the action of the piece.

Simon Callow, who had by now made his mark as a director (and biographer, actor, and restaurant critic) was enthusiastic about directing the script. We found a producer to option it for a West End production, and we set about finding a cast. At this point Tamas Szirtes of the Madach Theater in Budapest approached me about doing the play the following summer and, believing we would be open in London by then, I granted him permission.

The play was the most difficult of all my scripts to cast. It called for a leading man who could sing and two actresses who had to look alike. Despite hundreds of faxes between Simon and me and a rendezvous in New York to hold auditions, we never did find the right combination. I've found that there is a certain momentum to the progress of a production, and when we were unable to find the right cast this momentum was broken and the play was put on the shelf.

The Hungarians, however, persevered. Tamas, a man of great charm, and I met in London and he told me that the play would be the first commercial production in Hungary in seventy-five years. He said, "We are borrowing money from a bank, and if the play is a success we will pay them back with interest. It's a new system." I said, "Yes, it's called capitalism." He grinned and said, "Does that work?" I made a comme ci, comme ça gesture.

That summer Jill and I flew to Budapest to see the world pre-miere of a play of mine in a language I neither spoke nor under-stood. Since I was the guest of honor I was denied my usual release of pacing at the back of the theater and so, after a last nervous pee (if I had a dollar for every one of those ...), I squeezed into a seat and hyperventilated, waiting for the opening curtain. A few min-utes into the play a delicious feeling of relaxation spread through me: the cast was superb and the production had captured the dif-ficult tone of the piece to perfection. Jill whispered, "Maybe your plays *gain* something in the translation."

As the cast took their curtain calls, my blood pressure soared again when the applause turned to an enormous, steady, rhythmic clapping that I interpreted as disapproval. It was explained that this was called "iron clapping" and was only heard when an audi-ence *really* liked something. The play ran for three years under the title *The Man I Love*, and then the production was televised nation-wide. I recently viewed the tape, which brought back pleasant memories even though I still don't speak a word of Hungarian.

I'm sometimes asked how I can judge the quality of a produc-tion in a language I don't understand. One answer is that good act-ing is good in any language—which is also true of bad acting. It is also puzzling to some that I can even follow the text. I'm not exact-ly sure how I do this myself, but since most of my plays are come-dies the laughs are obvious markers, and I'm aware of the "beats" of the scenes in a good translation. Of course, the reaction of the audience usually is an indication of the quality of the production. I say "usually" because this is not always an accurate barometer. This was the case when I later attended a production in Berlin.

During the London rehearsals of *Fatal Attraction* we had bought a flat in Knightsbridge and ever since have spent at least two months of every year in England. These sojourns prompted my next play, which was a transatlantic comedy called *You Say*

Tomatoes and was written out of a desire to air all the aspects that bothered me about Britain and the United States. I chose to write it as a comedy because I'd remembered a quote by Bernard Shaw to the effect that "if you're going to tell the truth, you'd better make them laugh or they'll kill you!"

Living in England is pleasantly evocative for me as I'm constantly reminded of my roots, but the reasons why I was glad to leave the country in 1948 are still largely apparent. It seems to me that while America is perceived as the land of opportunity, Britain is the land of remembrance, where ambitions are limited by one's accent and background, and despite the appearance of social changes, the class system is still firmly in place. My major antipathy, though, is the quality of repression that is so ingrained in the British. This could be an overreaction on my part as I believe the worst part of my own personality was formed in England, and I have been known to sit next to someone on a plane for ten hours and not acknowledge their presence. This reticence, intense desire for privacy, shyness, or just plain unfriendliness shows itself in hundreds of smaller ways in the British character. For instance, the British do not put a return address on the outside of envelopes. God forbid that anyone should find out where they live. Obituaries never mention how a person died—they protect their privacy even in death. An English friend asked me why I would want to know the cause of death and I replied, "So I know what to watch out for."

Anti-Americanism in Britain is a curious mixture of envy and dismissiveness and can be found on almost every page of any newspaper. I am exposed to this perception in an undiluted form because our common background tends to make my old friends think of me as English and they don't bother to disguise their attitudes. I've lived in the States for over thirty-five years and have been appalled and amused by some of the national characteristics of that country as well. So, as a Canadian, I believed I enjoyed a unique vantage point to explore the virtues and foibles of both nationalities in a comedy guaranteed to offend everybody … and even provide a few laughs.

Sadly, the two countries are becoming quite similar, and fast food is not the only sinister element of American life that has drifted across the Atlantic. One Saturday night in London my wife and I couldn't get a taxi after seeing a play, so we wandered down the Strand to wait for a bus outside of Charing Cross station. Now, this is not the most salubrious area in the city late at night. Nevertheless, I felt quite safe and said, "You know what's great about London? You don't get the crazy street people like you do in New York." Right on cue, a sweet-looking, apple-cheeked elderly lady with tightly curled gray hair approached me and said, "Excuse me. May I smell your coat?" I thought I hadn't heard her correctly. "My what?" She repeated, "May I smell your coat?" All I could manage was a nod. She leaned over, took a deep sniff, smiled her thanks, and disappeared. At least her British nose was not as lethal as an American switchblade, but, yes, the world is getting smaller.

The writing of the play was fueled by a series of unrelated experiences in the summer of 1997 and, for a short time, changed me from being somewhat of an Anglophile to a full-fledged Anglophobe.

It started when we arrived in London to find that the ceiling in our flat had collapsed and the place looked like a blitzed building from World War II. "Tired plaster," they said it was. One hour later we discovered we had picked up the wrong suitcase at the airport, and two hours later Jill broke a cap on one of her front teeth. A half hour later we learned that an old friend, Mark Furness, whom I was supposed to see that day, had died. Supposedly a ruptured aortic valve, but I believe the British medical establishment did him in.

After days of drinking tea with assorted workmen, we got the ceiling fixed and Jill went off to take a three-week course in English literature at Oxford University. Two days later, dressed only in boxer undershorts and a pajama top, I was putting out the garbage on the landing of our five-unit building when I heard the chilling click of my flat door closing behind me. It was Saturday morning and everyone in the building had gone to the country, including the janitor. After racing up and down the stairs yelling for help, a woman eventually appeared on a landing. Dressed in a robe, of indeterminate age, and with a definite touch of Estelle Wynward about her, she invited me into her flat. Clutching a cushion over my gaping crotch, I sat on a stool in the kitchen as she tried to phone the janitor. It was then that I noticed odd sounds emanating from her person. Too loud to ignore, I asked her what they were and she opened her robe revealing a green parrot on her bosom. When he squawked, she said, "He gets very jealous when other men are around."

By this time, she had given up on finding the janitor and was trying to locate a locksmith. As she was doing this I noticed an odd thing: we were wearing the same pajamas. Marks and Spencers. No luck finding a locksmith, so both of us, wearing our twin pajamas, trooped upstairs to try and open my door with a credit card. No luck there, either. Some two hours later, after I'd heard her life story, she finally managed to locate a locksmith. A six-foot-six Jamaican, he double parked his van, bounded up the stairs, and, with a credit card and a flick of the wrist, opened my door. As I was writing out the check for a hundred and ten pounds (double time on Saturdays), he looked from me to my new friend, noted our matching pajamas, and said, "Is she your sister?"

Since this whole episode had its comic overtones, I naturally related it to Jill, who was still in Oxford. Two days later I was having breakfast in a small restaurant in Harrods department store. My bag, containing every important document I owned, was at my feet. I noticed two men studying me but didn't think much of it.

Then a pile of dishes was knocked over behind me and I glanced backwards. Ten minutes later, when I bent to retrieve my bag, I found it was gone. They ran up twenty-one thousand dollars on one credit card in forty minutes, mostly at jewelry stores around Harrods. I was not liable but have rarely been so angry. It wasn't a case of being "violated"—I suspect I would have enjoyed that—it was because this happened in *London*, which was supposed to be safe. Not true. I found out later that this sort of thing had happened to almost everyone I knew. The media just keeps it quiet. Anyway, I tried to get in touch with Jill in Oxford to tell her not to use her credit card. She didn't have a phone and the porter garbled the message when he passed it onto Jill. She thought that someone had broken into our flat, beaten me up, and robbed me. Possessing a vivid imagination, she believed it was the six-foot-six locksmith. Unable to reach me, she threw up on the immaculate lawn of Worcester College.

The misadventures weren't over. When I visited her in Oxford we stayed at the Randoph Hotel, where we were rousted out of bed at two o'clock in the morning and spent an hour in our bare feet on the damp pavement while they checked the fire alarm. The next day, while visiting a lovely old pub, I was bitten by a wasp ... again. I had been bitten two weeks before.

At that point the summer weather changed from drizzly rain to a heat wave, complete with the usual English summer humidity. No air-conditioning in our hundred-and-five-year-old building, of course, and what they call air-conditioning in restaurants was lukewarm. By now, the "British Museum had lost its charm" and we fled back to Los Angeles. I realize that it's not exactly rational to blame England for all these mishaps, but I wasn't in a mood to be logical. I eventually regained some affection for England and still spend time every year in London, but the affair is no longer passionate.

The first act of *You Say Tomatoes* takes place in a cottage in Sussex and the second act in an East Village apartment in New York. There are four characters in the piece, with the two leading roles being a reclusive English mystery writer and a loud, bawdy New York woman. The two characters were originally written to be in their late forties, but when Bea Arthur expressed an interest in the play, I rewrote them to be in their sixties. After a number of meetings with Bea we set about finding an English leading man. A number of highly respected actors who I thought would fit the bill were available, but, for reasons I was never able to ascertain, Bea wouldn't approve of any of them. After a lunch with one actor, she turned him down with the puzzling remark, "He has English teeth." Eventually, she lost interest in the play, which was a disappointment as I was looking forward to hearing her inimical delivery of the lines. The play languished until it was given a production in a small theater on Martha's Vineyard, where we often spent some of our summers.

I have a favorite scene in this play too, which I feel sums up the basic differences between the repressed Englishman, Giles, and the uninhibited American woman, Libby. The action that leads up to this scene is that Libby, a TV producer, has tracked down the reclusive Giles in order to try and get the rights to his mystery novels. During their first meeting all the animosity he harbors about the United States comes to the surface, and at the end of the evening they intensely dislike one another. The next morning, after some initial sparring, there relationship becomes more friendly.

(LIBBY *starts to get up from her chair, grimaces, and doubles over*)
LIBBY Oh shit!
GILES (*Alarmed*) What? What is it?
LIBBY A cramp—charley horse—my leg—please—grab my leg!
GILES I beg your ...

LIBBY For God's sake—just do it! (*He gingerly takes the calf of her leg in his hands*) No—harder—rub it harder—(*As he does*) yeah, that's good—a bit higher.

GILES Feeling better?

LIBBY I didn't finish my stretch exercises and—yeah, that's good, that feels good, yeah.

(*He stops massaging but still keeps his hand on her leg*)

GILES I'm glad. I know a cramp can be very——

(*He suddenly grabs her and kisses her. They break. She is covered with confusion. He does not show any visible reaction but, surprisingly, carries on talking as if nothing untowards has taken place*)——uh, painful. Of course, I was never one for strenuous sports. I went to (*She watches, absolutely dumbfounded as he moves away*) a number of different schools, mostly to avoid being ambushed by reporters who wanted to know about the state of my parents' marriage, but I was somewhat uncoordinated so I never became involved with (*LIBBY raises her hand, but he chooses not to see it*) sports. I'm afraid this made me rather the odd man out in school but ...

LIBBY Uh ... excuse me.

GILES Yes?

LIBBY Am I crazy or did some physical contact take place a few moments ago?

GILES Really?

LIBBY I'm almost positive. Are you trying to say it escaped your attention?

GILES Of course not. I ... I just thought it was bad form to bring it up.

LIBBY Bad form?

GILES Look, do we have to talk about it? I mean, can't we just pretend it? (*He suddenly kisses her again*) I'm—I'm terribly sorry. I don't know why it—I really am *terribly* sorry.

LIBBY (*Totally thrown*) Hey, it's okay. I mean—it's okay. (*He kisses her again. Flustered*) Does this mean I get the rights? (*He looks at her, unbelievingly*) Only kidding! Didn't mean it. Really—I'm a bit confused—I just can't put it all in my head yet.

GILES I know. I don't understand any of this either. I mean, I was never one to just let my physical urges to ... to rule my ... . (*He kisses her urgently*) My God, I can't believe this! I'm *old*!

LIBBY (*Breathlessly*) Well, it's nice that we finally found something we have in common.

GILES The point is, I don't have a clue about how to act in a circumstance like this. I mean, it's not even supposed to come up when one is this old. The situation I mean. Do *you* have any idea what to do about—it?

LIBBY Well, it's been a long time since I've actually *done* anything about it.

GILES It has?

LIBBY If I said my love life over the past few years has been meager, I'd be bragging.

GILES I find that hard to believe.

LIBBY Listen, I've almost forgotten where everything goes.

GILES What?

LIBBY Uh ... the noses ... that sort of thing.

GILES Oh yes, I know what you mean. Look, would you mind terribly if I ... (*He kisses her*) What next?

LIBBY Listen, I'm out of practice at this sort of thing—there's blood pounding in my head and ... look, even in my prime I was never exactly Madonna.

GILES Who?

LIBBY I never slept with anyone I hadn't had Thanksgiving dinner with. Look, would you do me a favor? Would you tell me to shut up before I ruin everything?

GILES I need some help.

LIBBY Well, if memory serves me we—uh—get a seedy room.

GILES We have one of those but—well, we'll have to wait until Daisy and Fred are asleep. Would that be all right?

LIBBY Absolutely.

GILES (*Kisses her, more gently this time*) Yes—well—I suppose we should rest up.

LIBBY Rest up? You think we should go into *training*?

GILES No, I just mean if we're going to have to stay up until … well, maybe we should take a nap.

LIBBY Oh, I'm too excited to sleep. It reminds me of when I was a kid, before the July the Fourth picnic. I could never sleep then either.

GILES You like picnics?

LIBBY Fireworks.

GILES Ah. Yes, see what you mean.

LIBBY Have I embarrassed you again?

GILES No, it's just that talking about something could lead to one being—disappointed.

LIBBY How?

GILES Well, one could be expecting rockets and only get a damp squib.

LIBBY That's okay. I'll settle for a damp squib. Listen, I'll settle for a damp anything.

(*He starts to laugh. She joins him and their laughter builds until they fall into each other's arms*)

The incident I particularly liked was him kissing her and then refusing to acknowledge it, and I was anxious to see this played in front of an audience.

I had nothing to do with the actual production but by now had developed a nervous system strong enough to actually watch an opening night. It was fraught. The leading man, an actor of advanced years, repeatedly "dried" during the performance. Now, most actors who forget their lines will ad-lib or invent some business until they get back on track. Not this poor chap, who would simply freeze for interminable moments. I left the theater with a sore head because every time he had gone up in his lines I had dug my fingers into my temples. Despite these heart-stopping pauses, I was pleased to see that the play seemed to hold together.

There was a sad postscript to this story. About a year later I received a letter from the actor in question with an abject apology for his not being able to remember the lines. He had since worked in a production of another play and had experienced the same problem. When he checked with a doctor it was discovered that he was suffering from the early stages of Parkinson's disease.

In 1998 the play was optioned by the Haymarket Theatre in Basingstoke, a small town about an hour and a half outside of London. I took the train down to meet Adrian Reynolds, the artistic director, who was going to direct the production. After I returned to the States, the theater went through the usual casting frustrations, but the project seemed to be on schedule, until two weeks before rehearsals were set to begin, when Adrian Reynolds dropped dead. Still only in his early fifties, I have never found out the exact cause of his death, but the tragic event threw everyone at the theater into a state of turmoil.

An American director, David Taylor, who resided in England, agreed to do the play, even though he had recently broken his leg and was hampered by a heavy white cast. After dozens of transatlantic casting conferences, the play was partially cast with Christopher Timothy, an actor best known for the TV series about vets called *All Things Bright and Beautiful*, a well-known character actor, Moray Watson, and a young actress, Emma Davies. The leading lady role was still not filled when I flew to London for rehearsals, which had been delayed a week. A day before the first rehearsals started it was decided to hire Susan Jameson, who in the past had often played hard-faced north-country women, for the role of Libby, a funny, loud, quintessential New Yorker. Not a marriage made in casting heaven.

At the end of the first day of rehearsals it was obvious that this piece of casting was more grievous than we'd imagined. Nobody's fault, certainly not that of the actress, but another factor surfaced. Apparently, she hated everything American, had trouble saying anything "bad" about England, and, in short, seemed to represent everything I was poking fun at about the British in the play. Christopher, on the other hand, *loved* everything about America, which was diametrically opposed to the beliefs of his character. This didn't affect his playing of the role, but it was an odd situation. However, it was too late to get another actress, so we "soldiered" on, forced to listen to a variety of really bad American accents from our leading lady. For this privilege I was having to spend four hours a day in dismal railway carriages and stations as I commuted to London. I felt as if I was in the middle of the movie, *Brief Encounter*, but without the comfort of bath buns or Celia Johnson.

The production staggered on (in more ways than one, as David dragged his huge cast around) towards the opening, which, after viewing the dress rehearsal, I decided to forego. Members of my family did attend and they quite liked the show … possibly because I'd filled their ears with dire predictions … but were puzzled to see that, because of a box office mix-up, the first ten rows of the orchestra had not been sold. I believe it was the "theater cat" in *Archibald and Mehitable* who said, "The theater is being ruined by amateurs!"

All of the plays from this period survived and went on to other productions, providing me with a magic carpet to cities and countries I might never have visited and giving me the opportunity to make some interesting new friends.

★ Same Time Another Year: the sequel ★

Over the years I had been approached a few times to write a sequel to *Same Time, Next Year* but had always declined, thinking it was wise not to push my luck. Then, some twenty years after the first production, I heard a statistic that *Same Time, Next Year* was the most produced two-character play in history. Of course, I was aware of its enormous popularity from my royalty statements but hadn't realized it was quite that pervasive. This fact started me thinking that the hundreds of companies who had presented the original would be interested in following it with a sequel. I was quite aware that sequels are almost never as successful as the originals, but this was not really a deterrent: I knew it would be too much to expect that the second play match the popularity of the first, so I felt no pressure to "top" it.

However, the main factor that nudged me into writing *Same Time Another Year* was that I tend to write characters who are the same age as myself. George and Doris would go from their early fifties to their mid-sixties in the sequel and I believed this age span would give me the chance to share some of the problems we face as we move into the third act of our lives. I started writing the play while on Martha's Vineyard (the fact that the first play was started in Hawaii, another island, was not lost on me) and, because I was so familiar with the characters, I had a first draft within weeks. The play was more autumnal than the first, but I thought that appropriate and, all in all, was quite happy with it.

Frankly, I believed that this would be the easiest of all my plays to get produced. I was mistaken. I had worked without an agent for some time, but because there were a number of new producing organizations on Broadway I decided the play needed an experienced representative to help find a production. The first jolt was when one of New York's best-known agents declined to handle it because "Broadway wasn't doing plays like this anymore."

I've learned to never take "no" for an answer—especially the first "no"—so I sent the play to Jimmy Nederlander, who offered to produce it at the Brooks Atkinson, where *Same Time, Next Year* was first presented. This appealed to my sense of symmetry, and I was hoping to underscore this feeling of continuity by casting actors who had played in the original. Unfortunately, most of the actors who had appeared on Broadway in the play were unavailable, too old, or, sadly, dead. The situation was complicated because Jimmy Nederlander wanted major stars (yeah, that old thing again) and pressed to hire a young director who must have been one of the few people in show business who hadn't seen the original. What's more, he didn't want to see the original as it might "spoil his vision" (yeah, that old thing again), so I sent the play to Simon Callow, who agreed to direct it. This didn't help, and we wasted a couple of years going down dead ends, including an extended pre-production period with a Toronto producer who had the bad taste (and timing) to lose millions of dollars and her backers in a musical performed just before our play was due to be presented. Eventually, I signed a contract with the Pasadena Playhouse to do the play, starring Barbara Rush and Tom Troupe under my direction. Tom and Barbara had played in the national company of *Same Time, Next Year* for close to two years, and since we had almost a year to iron out any problems with the script before the start of rehearsals, I couldn't foresee any problems. We had three readings, which bolstered my confidence in the material, and Tom and Barbara took daily walks during which they learned the lines. Everything proceeded smoothly until about three weeks before the start of rehearsals, when life (yeah, that old thing again) interfered.

I'm not going to presume that a personal experience in Barbara's life caused her changes in attitude, but she had been reading the script for over a year so something must have happened to cause her to announce that she didn't want to play any scene that had anything to do with her character getting older. Since the play dealt specifically with the process of aging, this created quite a problem. But I reluctantly agreed to eliminate any references to the actual age of her character. She then objected to scenes dealing with illness and attacked the play for being depressing. Actually, the scenes she criticized turned out to be the funniest in the play (but she couldn't recognize this until she came to see a performance after we'd opened).

Then came the capper. One situation that is impossible to deal with is when an actor criticizes dialogue by saying, "I wouldn't say that." This means that they've lost sight that the character is not written as them. This book is not intended as a primer for young playwrights, but let me pass on one piece of advice: when an actor starts saying that, head for the nearest bar! Barbara and I decided to part ways.

We were now left without a leading lady only ten days before rehearsals were scheduled, but we got lucky. Nancy Dussault, even though she was performing in *Candide* at night at the Ahmanson Theater, agreed to do double duty and rehearse with us during the day. Apart from her talents as a singer, Nancy is a gifted comedienne and I quickly rewrote the script to take advantage of her impeccable comic timing and clowning abilities. She was without any time-wasting temperament and since she was willing to work until she dropped, the rehearsals were as much fun as a two-character play's rehearsals can be—which is not a lot. This is because the work on a two-hander is extremely intense and both physically and emotionally draining on the actors. It also poses special demands on the director, as all the reactive energy must come from him (or, of course, her) since he is the one person the actors look to for constant reassurance. I find demonstrating enthusiasm for the work being done absolutely exhausting, no matter how good and deserving of admiration the work is.

There is another major drawback in directing one's own work. The writer has already spent a number of years on the play before the start of rehearsals, so it is much less a "voyage of discovery" for him than for the actors. With this stimulus missing there is the danger that watching endless rehearsals will induce acute boredom. This, of course, must be hidden from the actors at all costs, but the strain of always being a cheerleader/coach is often enervating. This is why some directors constantly make changes in the blocking or characterization just to keep themselves from going crazy. This practice can be dangerous as it often diminishes the original intent of the piece.

Given the tediousness of directing my own work I am sometimes asked why I elect to do it. The answer is simple: it is much less stressful dealing directly with actors, when I can at least try to communicate what I had in mind, than having to go through the third person of a director and trust that my thoughts will be translated accurately. I chose to direct *Same Time Another Year* because it was the first production, I knew the characters better than anyone, and if the play failed I wanted to be sure that I could blame only myself. But it is not something I want to make a habit of doing.

The Pasadena Playhouse has a luxurious rehearsal period followed by ten previews, which gives everyone the time to make any necessary adjustments. I did make some cuts and rewrote the beginning slightly, but *Same Time Another Year* played smoothly from the first preview. The enjoyment of the audience was palpable, and it was the only one of my plays that made me confident enough to mingle with the crowd during intermission and not be afraid of overhearing anything negative. The average age of the Pasadena ticket buyers coincided with those of the onstage characters, and it was evident from their reactions that many had experienced some of the situations presented in the play. One gratifying aspect peculiar to the production was that many audience members would come backstage after the performances, not to collect autographs, but to satisfy a need to talk about the play. Although the piece touched on some of the more somber aspects of growing older, not only did it not depress the audience but seemed rather to send them away with a spring in their step.

A writer learns to avoid the use of coincidences in writing fiction narrative, but real life has no such qualms. One night, while standing in the wings and half listening to the performances in progress, I became aware that the two actors onstage had stopped speaking. The stage manager told me that he believed it was because a man in the first few rows of the orchestra seemed to be having a heart attack. I was urged to speak to the audience to calm them down, so I announced that a man was having a health problem but that I was sure a doctor would soon be available to help take care of the situation. At this point a man leaned over the balustrade of the balcony, spotted the man below who was in trouble, and said, "I'm his doctor!" This, in a thousand-seat theater at a specific performance of a ten-week run. Charles Dickens would have trouble selling that! There was a happy ending: the man was not having a heart attack but was bothered by something he had eaten (not, I'm glad to say, by something I'd written) and came back later in the week to see the play again.

★ 211 ★

In the spring of that year a German-language production of the play opened at the Komodie Theater in Berlin, and I was told it was a big hit. Almost all of my plays have been produced in Germany, but since Jill and I had never actually been there, we decided to fly to Berlin the following October to see this latest production. Well, indeed it was a huge success. The audience laughed their heads off and the cast of two took some fourteen curtain calls. It was also a truly ghastly production. Horrendous set, awful costumes, ludicrous wigs, really stupid direction, and a cast who overacted so badly they could only be appreciated by people who think that Jim Carrey "holds back too much." Now, this sort of misguided presentation is sometimes to be expected if the playwright is not around to protect his work, but what was unforgivable was that the director and theater owner, one Jurgen Wölffer, had elected to add fifteen to twenty minutes of incomprehensible film clips, posters, and tapes of unrecognizable music not only between the scenes but even after the house's lights had gone down before the start of the play. To accommodate his theatrical genius he had cut the same amount of time from the actual text. At the curtain call I was asked to take a bow. I simply rose and, with my hands in front of my face, like a Mafia don who didn't want to be photographed, stumbled from the theater.

It had been arranged for the entire company to host a party for us in some restaurant in East Berlin, where I proceeded to drink heavily and was kept from erupting by my wife, who had her hand painfully clamped to my thigh to prevent any unpleasantness. Eventually, in a *very* tight voice, I calmly enumerated all my objections to the production but was met with blank stares and the baffled reply, "But how do you know all this? You do not speak German." I explained that I had seen plays of mine presented all over the world and that I could spot the grubby, untalented hands of a director in any language. I asked Wölffer why the Germans had no comedy writers of their own. He said, "Because we have no sense of humor." By now on my fifth vodka, I said, "Maybe that's because you killed all your Jews." Silence. *Dead* silence. Jill and I moved to the door where, unable to resist an exit line, I added, "And tonight you started on the Gentiles." This perfect evening was capped by my elderly agent, Stephanie Hunzinger, being mugged outside the theater. This created a strong bond between us as I had been mugged *inside* the theater.

There was a bittersweet second act. The company had scheduled a forty-week tour of the play after the Berlin run, but I told them that not only was I closing the show in Berlin but that I was withdrawing the rights for the tour. I could do this because my contracts stipulate that the text cannot be altered. There was much pulling of the hair and how-can-you-do-thats, but I remained firm. German royalties are quite lucrative and if I'd been a struggling young playwright I might not have taken such a strong action, but I felt I was striking a blow, however glancing, for all playwrights. Some months later, I received a new translation of the play, which was scheduled for a production in Munich.

A few years later (in the theater these things take time), and after two options that didn't result in productions, the play was eventually presented by Bill Kenwright in a production starring Paula Wilcox and Dennis Waterman, who had previously starred in *Same Time, Next Year.*

The production was directed by Roger Redfarn. I had first met Roger when he directed *Romantic Comedy* for the English Speaking Theatre in Vienna. I was amused by the unique situation of having an English cast play an American play for Austrians who speak English, but the experience I remember most from Vienna took place away from the theater. I was staying in a luxurious hotel and one day, while lolling in the very grand bathtub, I was idly playing with a cord on the wall that I assumed was intended for people who wanted to dry their lingerie. Without warning, the door crashed open and a hefty man and a woman burst in and proceeded to try and pull me out of the bathtub. Out of the corner of my eye I noticed a small sign by the cord that read "SOS," and I realized it was an alarm for anyone having a heart attack. Neither of my "helpers" spoke English and wouldn't take "nein" for an answer. While they were struggling with my naked body a small part of my brain was trying to figure out how I could get this scene on stage. Once a writer ...

I caught up with the British production of *Same Time Another Year* in the charming theater of Windsor, one of the weekly pre-London engagements on an extended tour. The management booked a seat for me at the Saturday matinee, but, not knowing that I never see a play of mine sitting down because I'm too afraid I'll overhear anything negative, they had put me in a seat right in the middle of the stalls, or what the Americans call the orchestra. Although I had heard good things about the production from friends and family, I still had some trepidation as the curtain went up. At the end of the first scene a man seated next to me turned to his wife and said in a gruff voice, "Well, this is not at all what I expected!" There was a longish pause as I inched down in my seat, and then he said, "This is *wonderful*!"

Paula and Dennis *were* quite wonderful, realizing every laugh but also catching the emotional quality of the piece, which, judging by the moist eyes around me, had a palpable effect on the audience. I later traveled to Brighton to see the play there and enjoyed the performance just as much as the first time. It appealed to my sense of nostalgia to be watching a play of mine in the very town where I had first fallen in love with the theater some fifty-odd years before. This nostalgia was heightened when I discovered that the woman seated next to me was Dame Vera Lynn, the singer who had popularized all those ballads of World War II and to whom I had listened when I was a small evacuee.

As I had surmised, the play has become very much in demand and over twenty productions in the States and around the world are planned.

Another magic carpet, just as my old one was wearing thin.

★ Listening to myself talk

Whenever I launch into an oft-told anecdote, I am usually cut short by my family who, over the years, have developed the distressing habit of raising their fingers to indicate how many times they've heard it. At first, this was done almost apologetically ... two or three fingers discreetly raised, hardly even noticeable by anyone outside the family circle, but lately the gestures have become shamelessly overt: ten fingers punched in the air, followed by a rapid succession of ten more fingers, and ten more, rather like a pianist limbering up his hands before playing. This nasty habit has been passed down to my small grandchildren, who, I suspect, must have been coached as it seems highly unlikely that at their young age they could have heard *all* my stories. One of the reasons, then, for writing this book is so I will never again have to confront a sea of fluttering fingers.

Another reason is that I finally had the time to work on something I was intensely interested in (me!) without having to worry if there would be a large financial reward. While writing plays over the past few years I was aware that the number of producers who were willing to produce new plays was shrinking, but I didn't realize how bad the situation was until I phoned my agent and said, "I'm thinking of writing a new play, but I don't know who to send it to." He said, "No, neither do I." This was my *agent*!

This caused me to consider other ways to fill my time. One obvious solution was teaching. One problem: I'm not at all sure that writing can be taught, believing that the only way to become a writer is to write. And rewrite. I do think that an objective party can make some useful comments on already written material, but this function also has some built-in dangers, as I believe it is not so much what the criticisms are but when they are made. Harsh criticism made too early can easily kill a promising idea. Both our children, Christopher and Laurie, are writers ... he a magazine editor and novelist and she a screenwriter ... so as reluctant "first-time" readers Jill and I are very much aware of the importance of timing when giving advice. The other major pitfall in trying to guide a young writer is that one has to studiously avoid the trap of telling him or her how *you* would have written it.

Over the years I've lectured at Columbia University, NYU, UCLA, University of Toronto, and Boston University and, with the possible exception of some classes of graduate film students, I am disconcerted not by the scarcity of talent (because talent is always rare) but by the lack of knowledge about the history of the entertainment business.

This does not apply just to students. I once "pitched" an idea for a television series to a network executive and said, "This is rather like a contemporary version of *The King and I*." She said, "What's *The King and I*?" I was reduced to asking, "Don't you remember the guy with the bald head?" She said, "Oh, you mean Telly Savalas." This was a woman in charge of comedy at a major network. I have a theory about this sort of ignorance. I think that a great many of the executives now are recruited MBAs, not graduates of liberal arts programs. It's the money that attracts them. Why go into Wall Street when you can make trillions in movies and also get to meet beautiful women and men?

Case in point. At one of my lectures I spent an hour carefully outlining all the complexities of adapting plays into films. After my rather erudite explanation, I called for questions and a young man in the first row shot up his hand. His question? "How much money do you make?"

Of course, not all students are like that, and there are many who really want to learn. One of the most unusual lectures I gave was to the Drama students at Boston University. I was trying out a new play that was going well, so when I was asked to speak one morning I agreed. I was scheduled to give my talk in a very large auditorium, but when I arrived I was somewhat chagrined to find only about fifteen people there in the first couple of rows. However, a promise is a promise so I launched into my lecture. As I spoke I noticed various people tiptoe into the auditorium, bend over an empty seat, and then quietly leave. Finally, I stopped and asked what the hell was going on. It was apologetically explained that there had been a mix-up and that they had scheduled me while the dress rehearsal of the major drama of the year was taking place. The students didn't want to miss my talk so had come in and put tape recorders on the seats. I was playing to about a hundred tape recorders! Hard to get laughs from that audience ... but at least they cared.

Like most produced playwrights, I am often asked what is the best training to become a writer. I can tell you everything I know in one paragraph. First, throw away all those "how-to" books, which tell you that you must have an "illuminating incident" on page seven and a "character revelation" on page twenty-seven, because they're useless. Much better to read every play or screenplay, past and present, you can lay your hands on. And see everything. I mean everything ... plays, musicals, movies, operas, ballets, and television shows—because this will not only help you to develop some taste but can inspire you to write for two different reasons: if something you see is bad you will think, "I can do better than that," and if it's marvelous, you will want to try to produce something as good. Also, join a theater group and do some acting, because you need to know how things "play." It will bring you into contact with like-minded people.

How do you get started? Through tenacity, passion, discipline, contacts, and luck. And don't discount any life experiences because careers can be started in the most surprising ways. When my son, Chris, was growing up all he seemed to think about was sports and he seemed to me to have a longer career in little league than Hank Aaron did in the majors. I like sports myself but was somewhat concerned about how all this tennis, baseball, and basketball was going to help him in a career. When he graduated from college he decided he wanted to go into publishing and managed to get two separate interviews at Doubleday. He struck out both times. He took a temporary job at Crown Books. They had a softball team and when they played the Doubleday team, Chris hit two home runs. The next morning he got a call from Doubleday wanting to hire him! He phoned me and said, "I'm not sure if they want me as an editor or if I've been drafted!"

Anyway, I decided I didn't want to settle for a seat in the grandstand yet and opted to persevere in my career as a playwright, although it increasingly seemed akin to being a nineteenth-century buggy maker. In the past, I have felt sorry for workers in show business whose world was taken away from them. Gifted musical comedy performers who came into their prime just as classic Broadway musicals were going out of fashion, singers, writers, and directors of TV variety shows who spent years honing their crafts only to see that form of entertainment discontinued, are all too familiar victims of the changing entertainment world. But I never believed that this unhappy circumstance would affect playwrights. There would always be a place on Broadway for the well-crafted straight play, wouldn't there? I'm afraid not.

Lately Broadway has been populated almost exclusively by big budget, special effects–oriented musical spectacles. The cost of these shows has effectively shut out the individual producers with a passion for a play, and they have been replaced by consortiums fueled by money. The few straight plays that do land a spot on Broadway are usually imported from England or begin their journeys in regional theaters not favorably disposed to the middle-of-the-road works that were once the staple of New York theater. Some plays are still produced off-Broadway but tend to be aimed at audiences with a taste for the esoteric, and American playwrights with a talent for creating "popular" plays of universal appeal have found that their once thriving marketplace has disappeared. It is no wonder that young writers who, years ago, would have devoted their talents to the theater have turned to television or film.

Robert Anderson has written that he has a sign over his desk that reads, "Nobody asked you to be a playwright." I'm not complaining, either, and I feel fortunate that I managed to get in under the wire to be part of that exciting world of New York theater that inspired me to write plays. But I miss Broadway ... both as an audience and as a contributor. Oh well, it was great while it lasted.

Luckily, there is still a place for the kind of plays I write in the "boulevard" theaters of Europe. The English theater in particular still offers a wide selection of entertainment, ranging from classics at one end of the spectrum to trouser-dropping farces at the other ... a healthy democratic diet of something for everyone. Anyway, my hand is always mentally out for a suitcase, and I'm always grateful for the use of the hall.

Not long ago, I was walking to the Cape Playhouse in Dennis, Massachusetts, to see the second act of a play of mine but stopped when I heard the sound of an audience's laughter emanating from the theater and floating across the surrounding fields. This shared laughter made the trip worthwhile. Not only that trip but my entire journey in the theater.

Index